The Icing on the Cake

SEE HOW THE INGREDIENTS
FIRST CAME TOGETHER!

Kitchen Chaos

the SATURDAY COOKING CLUB

The Icing on the Cake

Deborah A. Levine *and* JillEllyn Riley

ALADDIN

NEW YORK   LONDON   TORONTO   SYDNEY   NEW DELHI

ALADDIN

An imprint of Simon & Schuster Children's Publishing Division
1230 Avenue of the Americas, New York, NY 10020
First Aladdin hardcover edition September 2015
Text copyright © 2015 by Deborah A. Levine and JillEllyn Riley
Jacket illustration copyright © 2015 by Annabelle Metayer
Also available in an Aladdin M!X paperback edition.
All rights reserved, including the right of reproduction in whole or in part in any form.
ALADDIN is a trademark of Simon & Schuster, Inc.,
and related logo is a registered trademark of Simon & Schuster, Inc.
For information about special discounts for bulk purchases, please contact
Simon & Schuster Special Sales at 1-866-506-1949 or business@simonandschuster.com.
The Simon and Schuster Speakers Bureau can bring authors to your live event. For more information or to book an event, contact the Simon & Schuster Speakers Bureau at 1-866-248-3049 or visit our website at www.simonspeakers.com.
Jacket designed by Jessica Handelman
Interior designed by Mike Rosamilia
The text of this book was set in Arno Pro.
Manufactured in the United States of America 0815 FFG
2 4 6 8 10 9 7 5 3 1
Library of Congress Cataloging-in-Publication Data
Levine, Deborah A., author.
The icing on the cake / by Deborah A. Levine and JillEllyn Riley.—First Aladdin hardcover/paperback edition. pages cm.—(The Saturday cooking club; #2)
Summary: "Liza's thirteenth birthday has been hijacked by her Nana Silver, who wants to throw her granddaughter a party more suited for a society page then the low-key celebration Liza wants. Can Liza's friends from the Saturday Cooking Club find the right recipe and ingredients to save the day?"—Provided by publisher.
[1. Birthdays—Fiction. 2. Friendship—Fiction. 3. Cooking—Fiction.]
I. Riley, JillEllyn, author. II. Title.
PZ7.1.L487Ic 2015
[Fic—dc23]
2014046623
ISBN 978-1-4424-9942-3 (hc)
ISBN 978-1-4424-9943-0 (pbk)
ISBN 978-1-4424-9944-7 (eBook)

For J, who's even yummier than dessert.
And for Sophie and Nora, the sweetest early reviewers
an author could ask for. —DAL

To M & M & M, the HP Girls,
for taking part in all the adventures—culinary
and otherwise—and constantly proving the power
of making things from scratch. —JER

CHAPTER 1

Liza

Thirteen. Thir-teen. 13. Even the word sounds unlucky. I'm not a big believer in superstitions, but my thirteenth birthday is still two months away and so far everything about it is bad news.

I used to love birthdays. As soon as one birthday party was over, I'd be on the phone with Frankie planning the next. My birthday's in March, so you never know what the weather will be like, and we usually have my parties indoors. But last year, when I turned twelve, I had an ice-skating party in Prospect Park and it was perfect—still cold enough so the rink didn't get all slushy, but plenty of sun and hot chocolate to warm us up. Earlier that winter my grandmother came to visit from Georgia and taught me to knit, and I made ten ear-warmer headbands all by myself for party favors. They weren't perfect—if you looked close enough you could see a lot of places where I dropped a stitch, and I had to start some of them over a few times—but my mom helped me finish them off so that the seams looked totally professional.

This year I wanted to do something small, but really special—just Frankie, Lillian, and me. We've been dying to go to Bubble Kingdom, this giant spa with fifteen hot tubs all at different temperatures, and a whole floor of special saunas with names like Crystal Muscle Relax and Soothing Color Treatment. There's even a cold sauna with ice and snow on the walls, according to Lillian's sister, Katie, who went to Bubble Kingdom with her track team. And on the roof, there's an outdoor pool that's always warm— even in the winter—with jets in the water that push you along while you're floating, like the current in a river.

It looks like Bubble Kingdom's going to have to wait till another birthday, though, since my unlucky thirteenth has been hijacked by my other grand- mother, Nana Silver. I know that sounds weird—how can someone else take over *my* birthday?—but if you knew Nana Silver, you'd understand. It all started over winter break, when my little brother, Cole, and I went to California to visit our dad, where he lives now since the divorce. Cole's only two and a half, so Nana "volunteered" to fly with us from JFK to LAX— even though my dad promised me on our last trip that the next time we visited I could babysit Cole on the plane myself (and earn thirty bucks in the process).

I love my Nana, but spending time with her can be sort of . . . well . . . exhausting. Nothing is ever exactly the way she wants it, and she's not shy about letting anyone—or everyone—know it. First, she gave the flight attendant a lecture about putting too much ice in her Diet Coke, and then another one for not asking if Cole and I were allergic to peanuts before offering them to us (even though we're not). She didn't like the route the taxi driver took to my dad's house, so she only tipped him two dollars (Dad knows her well enough to have had his wallet with him when he came out to meet us, and he slipped the driver some more cash when Nana wasn't looking).

There's a pool at my dad's apartment complex— how cool is that? Not cool enough for Nana Silver, apparently. One day she complained to the lifeguard that there was too much chlorine in the water, and the next day she told him she saw algae growing near the ladder and she wouldn't be surprised if all the children who'd been swimming got sick. Dad's pretty much used to her by now, and Cole's too little to be embarrassed by anything, but when Nana starts complaining about things in public, I wish I could just melt into my seat or sink to the bottom of the pool.

Acting bossy to people just trying to do their jobs wasn't how Nana sabotaged my birthday plans, though. Instead, she activated her superpower: the ability to lay on an impenetrable guilt trip. Even my dad, who knows all of her tricks, is powerless in the face of Nana's giver-of-guilt abilities. But he put up an impressive fight for three and a half days. Usually, Nana tries to make her only son feel bad about getting divorced and moving thousands of miles away from all of us (especially from Cole, who was just one when Dad took his job in LA). Not this time. On this trip, she surprised us all with a brand-new reason to make my dad feel guilty—*me*.

"Liza must be so disappointed," Nana said to Dad at dinner on our first night in LA. I was putting ketchup on my hamburger and froze midsqueeze.

My dad looked at me curiously, but I had no idea what Nana was talking about. So I just shrugged.

"About what?" he asked.

Nana threw up her hands as if the answer was completely obvious. "Turning thirteen without a bat mitzvah, of course. You're depriving her of her heritage—not to mention a fabulous party." I nearly choked on my burger.

A bat mitzvah is a big event for Jewish girls when they turn thirteen (boys have bar mitzvahs). You practice for it for at least a year, and then you get up in front of the entire synagogue, your whole family, your friends, your parents' friends, your grand-parents' friends—you get the idea—and recite a lot of stuff in Hebrew. When it's over, you've officially become "an adult"—or at least that's what it meant, like, a thousand years ago. Most families throw a big party afterward—my cousin Phoebe had a DJ and a photo booth at hers. But unlike Nana Silver, most people don't decide to do this only three months before their kid turns thirteen.

"She's only half Jewish, Mom." Dad sighed. "Jackie

and I made a decision a long time ago not to raise the kids one religion or the other. You know that. We give them a little bit of both, and they can choose for themselves when they get older—or not."

Nana is a champion eye-roller. "That was all fine and good when she was little, Adam, but now that she's coming up on thirteen, it just seems like such a shame." (Actually, it was never fine and good with Nana—but that's another story.)

"It's okay, Nana," I jumped in, feeling bad for my dad. "Really. I don't want a bat mitzvah—I don't even go to Hebrew school."

"You don't need to remind me of that," Nana said, shaking her head as if not sending me to Hebrew school was like shipping me off to join a gang.

"Besides," I added, "I don't even want a big party. Frankie and Lillian and I have been planning a totally amazing spa day for months."

Nana waved me off like I hadn't even been talking. "You don't even know what you'd be missing," she said. Then she turned back to my dad and pointed at him with a frosty-pink fingernail. "But she will in a few years, Adam, and she'll resent you for it."

Nana went on like this for three days, nagging my dad about this "neglect" or that "lost opportunity" every chance she got. On our fourth day in LA, we spent the morning doing a movie-studio tour. It was supposed to be just Dad and me, so we could spend some QT together and catch up. But Cole was acting cranky about staying at the apartment with Nana (can you blame him?), so the two of them ended up tagging along. After a stunt show and a tour of the 3-D animation lab, we stopped at the studio café for lunch. My little brother *loved* seeing all of his favorite cartoon characters come to life at the animation lab and spent a solid hour acting totally hyper—which meant he was passed out in his stroller before his chicken tenders even arrived. With Cole asleep, Nana was able to focus her full attention on bugging Dad about my "not mitzvah."

"Look at her," Nana said as I sipped my iced tea. She was talking to Dad but smiling at me in this very Nana Silver-ish way that told me she was about to lay on the guilt. "Such a lovely young lady—so grown up." I could feel myself starting to blush and was relieved when she turned to my dad. "Yet for some reason her father doesn't think she's worth celebrating."

Dad let the roll he'd started buttering drop onto the table. "That's a ridiculous accusation, Mom, even for you," he said. "Of course I think Liza's worth celebrating—I celebrate everything about her." If your blush can blush, mine did right then. "We're just not going to be celebrating at the bat mitzvah she is not going to have."

"I understand that," Nana said. "Even if I don't like it. Still, she's coming of age, Adam. She'll only turn thirteen once. Is it so wrong for me to want to recognize this milestone in my only granddaughter's journey to womanhood?" Oh my God, I had to grip the seat of my chair with both hands to keep myself from totally bolting.

"So what do you want me to do, Mom?" Dad ran his hands through his hair the way he does when he's really frustrated. "Throw Liza a Sweet Thirteen? You heard her—she and her friends already have birthday plans in the works."

"At this really fun place called Bubble Kingdom, Nana," I chimed in, giving her my best perfect-granddaughter smile. "We're all super excited—it's exactly what I want."

Nana raised her eyebrows. "Bubble Kingdom? I've heard of that place. It's for people who like to take baths in public with complete strangers."

I couldn't help myself—I laughed out loud. "It's a *spa*, Nana. And the department of health gave it the highest rating. Lillian checked."

"For your thirteenth birthday, you should be treated like the princess of your own kingdom—not soaking in other people's bathwater and sauna sweat."

"I think that's enough, Mom," my dad said.

Thankfully, the waitress arrived with our food. We were all silent for a few minutes while she served our meal and refilled water glasses.

"All right," Dad said, rubbing his hands together. "How about we table this conversation and eat our lunch in peace?"

Nana pushed her plate away. "I don't seem to have much of an appetite anymore."

"Suit yourself," Dad said, digging in to his turkey club.

I picked at my pasta salad, but I wasn't very hungry anymore either. We sat there like that for what seemed like forever—Dad chomping on his sandwich, Nana scowling, and me looking from one to the other and wishing I could trade places with Cole—until finally, I couldn't take it anymore.

"Bubble Kingdom can wait," I said. "I'll only turn thirteen once." I turned to my grandmother. "I'm not going to have a bat mitzvah, Nana, but I guess a bigger party could be kind of . . . um . . . fun."

I caught my dad's eye as Nana threw her arms around me. He looked surprised, but there was also something in his eyes that said, *Welcome to the club.* I guess Nana was right about me "coming of age"—I'm not too little for her guilt trips anymore.

The minute we got into the car to head back to my dad's place, I texted Frankie and Lillian.

U won't believe what happened, I typed. *HELP!*

CHAPTER 2
Liza

"I still don't get what you're so upset about," Frankie says as she finishes off a coat of royal-blue polish on her littlest toenail. We're all squeezed into the Caputos' upstairs bathroom with our feet propped up on the edge of every available surface. Lillian and I are doing each other's toes because neither of us is coordinated enough to polish our own, but Frankie's amazing at giving herself pedicures.

"What's not to get?" I ask, looking up from my spot

on the floor where I'm dunking a Q-tip in nail-polish remover to erase what was at least my sixth mess-up on Lillian's left foot. "Have you ever heard me say I wanted a big fancy party where everyone's going to be staring at me the whole time?"

Frankie has to bang the bottle of top-coat on the sink a few times to unstick the lid. "No, but it doesn't sound like the worst thing imaginable to me. Music . . . food . . . boys—what's so awful about that?"

"Yeah," says Lillian, who has been concentrating hard on the tiny yellow flowers she's painting on each of my nails. You wouldn't believe how many ways we've discovered that Lillian's artistic talent comes in handy. "You'll get to buy a new outfit, and everybody will be snapping pictures of you and showering you with attention—it'll be like you're a celebrity."

You would think that my two closest friends would be supportive no matter what, right? I guess I can't blame Lillian, because we've only known each other for a few months. But Frankie? Frankie and I have been BFFs since forever—"Like white on rice," my mom always says, meaning we're inseparable and know each other backwards and forwards. I was sure Frankie would immediately get how unpsyched I am about this big thirteenth birthday bash I somehow agreed to let Nana Silver throw for me. But for some reason both of my friends are acting like my unluckiest birthday ever could actually be *fun*.

"Guys," I say, probably sounding a little annoyed, "standing around in some froofy dress while everybody stares at me isn't my idea of a good time. I can't believe you don't know that!"

Frankie looks up from her toes. "Lize, I know you don't like being the center of attention, but that's kinda part of the deal when it's your birthday. You might actually enjoy yourself if we plan it right."

"But that's just it, Franks," I whine, scraping some dried-up pink polish off the floor. "We're not planning it. If we were, the three of us would be spending my birthday getting pruny in the tubs and sipping Hawaiian ices at Bubble Kingdom. Knowing Nana, she's probably already booking a party room and picking out tablecloths. And, as Mr. Mac would say, Nana Silver is *not* a 'good collaborator'!" Our social studies teacher, Mr. McEnroe, is really big on collaboration.

"Oh, come on," Frankie says. "Nana Silver's not that bad. It's not like she's going to make you wear glass slippers and ride to the party in a horse-drawn carriage or anything."

Lillian stops blowing on my toenails and looks up at us. "Although that would be pretty amazing," she says, in all seriousness. "Don't you think?"

Frankie and I look at each other and crack up. Lillian looks hurt for a minute, but then she laughs too. "Okay, so it's kind of Walt Disney. But it would still be cool to ride in a carriage. I've always wanted to."

Frankie waddles over to Lillian on her heels, careful not to mess up her still-wet polish. "You're a hopeless girlie-girl romantic, Lillian," she says, shaking her head. "But we love you anyway."

"Aww," I say as the two of them hug. I still can't help smiling and feeling relieved whenever Frankie does or says something nice to Lillian. It was super stressful back in the fall when we first met Lillian. Frankie acted like the Ice Queen around her all the time and she was always really put out whenever Lillian showed up. But she and Lillian have been getting along great ever since the Immigration Museum in Mr. Mac's class, when the three of us presented our project on the origins of so-called "American" food. Right before the big night, Frankie's mom, Theresa, accidentally set our homemade sourdough rolls on fire, and then one of her brothers smothered them with a fire extinguisher. Everything was ruined. Frankie almost lost her mind, but Lillian and Theresa saved the day by coming up with the idea to make waffle ice-cream cones. I think we had the most popular project at the museum thanks to them. Frankie decided Lillian was a keeper after that, and I was so glad not to be stuck in the middle anymore.

I'm warming my feet on the radiator when the phone rings. It's thirty-four degrees out with drifts of two-week-old dirty snow still bordering the sidewalk, but I wore flip-flops home on the bus so I wouldn't destroy my pedicure. So what if no one's going to see my toes for the next four months? My bright-pink nails with their perfect little flowers are enough to cheer me up on a slushy winter day.

"Liza, it's your dad," my mom calls from the kitchen where my phone is charging.

"Can you get it?" I ask, not yet ready to move my toes from the heater. "Please?"

"Hmm," my mom says, shaking her head, but she answers it anyway. "Her Highness is busy thawing her paws," she says, grabbing the phone and heading in my direction. She gets halfway across the room before she stops and scrunches up her eyebrows. "Really? What about?"

Instead of handing me the phone, my mom leans back on the arm of the couch. "Oh yeah," she says, looking at me, "Liza told me. Nana Silver strikes again."

Clearly, they're talking about the party.

"Of course I remember," Mom says, her lips curling up ever so slightly. "My cousin Denise still hasn't stopped talking about that chocolate fountain. At least your mother's wedding planning was a hit with our guests." Then my mom does something really weird, considering she's talking to my dad: she laughs.

"Anyway," she says, "I told Liza that I'll do my best to be supportive, but if Nana's running the show, I'm just going to step back and let her do her thing. If she goes too far—which we know she will—it's up to you, Daddy, to rein her in."

She laughs again. "Oh yes, I did say that. You

heard me right." She's practically bubbling. I give her a look, but she waves me off. "We'll see about that," she says into the phone, still chuckling.

Still smiling, my mom picks at a loose thread on the arm of the couch, not saying anything. Then, suddenly, she clears her throat. "Oh right, of course," she says, looking up at me, in her back-to-business voice. "She's right here, hang on."

Mom hands me the phone. "It's Dad."

"Um, thanks," I say. "I knew that."

I'm not sure what just happened, but it sounded to me like my mom and dad were actually enjoying talking to each other. If Mom was laughing and making jokes, I'm pretty sure Dad was too. Hmm . . . Maybe letting Nana plan my birthday party won't end up being the unluckiest thing that ever happened after all. . . .

CHAPTER 3

Liza

I'm watching *Antonio's Kitchen* for the first time in weeks—all of December was repeats, which is pretty boring when it's a cooking show, even if it is my favorite. *Antonio's Kitchen* has a new look for the new year. The set looks more modern, somehow, with shiny steel appliances and black-and-white subway tiles on the wall behind the stove. Here and there are splashes of red—the pots hanging from the wall, the tea towel thrown over Chef's shoulder—that keep things from looking too slick and fancy and matching. I imagine Chef Antonio pushing a giant update button and instantly upgrading the studio kitchen like it's an app on his phone.

I'm happy to see that Chef still looks like himself, though in this new studio he seems even more like a TV star than he did before. It's funny to think of him that way now that I "know" him, but it's been so many months since Frankie, Lillian, and I took his class with our moms that I bet he's forgotten all about us.

After the session ended last fall and Chef Antonio surprised us by bringing the entire cooking class to our middle school project night, we were supposed to all stay in touch and get together for a reunion over Thanksgiving weekend. But too many people had other plans, so we ended up rescheduling—and then rescheduling again—until suddenly it was the holidays, and everyone got even busier. We all exchanged e-mail addresses, but I guess it's like that old saying "out of sight, out of mind," because it's been weeks since I've heard from anyone. (Except Chef's son, Javier, who is our age and kind of hung out at our Saturday cooking class with us. Sometimes he texts Frankie, Lillian, and me stupid jokes or weird pictures he takes when he goes food shopping with his dad—he has a thing for trying to make the headless ducks hanging in Asian markets look artsy.)

The main ingredient on today's show is sweet potatoes. Chef Antonio has all kinds of plans for them: soup, chili, fries, a cheesy *gratin*, and, of course, pie. I wish my mom were here—she's a sweet-potato freak—but she's taking Cole for a booster shot right after daycare. I should be finishing my homework, but instead I'm having some leftover chicken pot pie and learning the difference between yams (they have skin that's usually darker than their flesh) and sweet potatoes (they're orange all over). Ever since we took the class, Mom has been on a roll, cooking all afternoon on Sundays so our fridge is stocked with meals we can just reheat and eat all week. I've actually been bringing my lunch to school rather than buying cafeteria glop, and even Frankie—whose dad packs her amazing stuff—can't keep her fork away from my food.

My phone buzzes. It's Lillian texting me and Frankie at the same time. She's watching *Antonio's Kitchen* too.

Chef looks HOT, Lillian says, which makes me laugh. If you only knew Lillian from her texts, that wouldn't be particularly funny. But Lillian in person is much sweeter and shyer than Virtual Lillian, and Frankie and I always crack up at how not-shy she comes off in her texts and e-mails.

Ikr. He's loving that new kitchen, I reply.

Yr mom watching? Frankie asks.

No, not home. Y? I type.

LOL. You know.

Know what? I'm starting to get annoyed.

I bet he's making her pie, Lillian writes.

What do u mean? I am really not enjoying this conversation with them.

Lize. That's Frankie. Lillian never uses nicknames. *U saw them flirting every week.*

My cheeks are suddenly burning and I'm glad they can't see me. Chef Antonio and my mom . . . flirting? I mean, they're definitely friendly, and there was that whole thing where Mom taught Chef to make noodle kugel, but that's not exactly flirting. Is it?

On TV, Chef grabs some dough and a rolling pin and I turn up the volume.

"For this pie, I'm using an old recipe that was given to me by a new friend," he says. "*Una amiga muy bonita.*" I'm only in my second year of Spanish, but even a first-semester sixth-grader could understand "a very beautiful friend."

OMG. Frankie again. *Lillian is right!*

GTG. I type, then immediately call my mom.

She picks up without saying hello. "Good timing. Dr. Gordon just gave your brother a Batman

Band-Aid and an ice pop. He only cried for seventeen minutes this time."

I wasn't in the mood to chat about Cole and his needle-phobia. "Mom, did you know Chef Antonio was making your sweet-potato pie on TV right now?"

"Really?" She sounds surprised, but pleased. "Good thing his show doesn't air in Georgia— Momma would be furious with me for sharing her secret recipe."

"So, like, you've been keeping in touch with Chef?" I ask her. "Lately, I mean?"

"Actually, I saw him when I stopped by the studio the other day, Lize."

"Really? Why?" I don't like this, not one bit.

"Antonio invited me to see the new studio design. Nice, huh?"

"Yeah, it looks really shiny. Why didn't you tell me you saw Chef?"

"Well, I was planning on keeping it a surprise."

This is getting weird. "Keeping what a surprise?"

"Well, I guess I have to tell you now, Liza Lou. I signed us up for Chef Antonio's next class—as an early birthday present. And I talked to Frankie's and Lillian's moms, and they're up for taking it too. Can you believe it? So we can all go together again! Exciting, right?"

Instantly, I feel myself relax—I hadn't even realized I'd gotten so worked up! My mom's been talking to Chef because she signed us up for another class. That's not exactly flirting! Frankie and Lillian have romance on the brain.

I hang up with Mom and text them again.

U guys are clueless. But I <3 u anyway.

CHAPTER 4
Frankie

Feng shui. Every time I'm at Lillian's house, all I can think about is *feng shui*. Not that I really know what that means, exactly, but I've seen it in magazine articles about where to put the couch, or which direction your bed should face. I'm pretty sure it's more than that, though, like at Lillian's, where everything is calm, peaceful, neat, and—I think this is the right word—*serene*. Beyond how ridiculously clean her house is, beyond the totally amazing food that her mom is always cranking out to make us feel welcome, there's also just this feeling you get when you're there, a sense of . . . I don't know . . . balance? Like things are as they should be.

I know Lillian feels like she has to live up to her mom's expectations. And with a sister like hers, those expectations must be set pretty high. But at her house I always feel like everything is right with the world and we can all take a deep breath. Maybe that's not what *feng shui* means. All I know is that there's something about Lillian's house that's the perfect antidote to mine.

We're scarfing down pot-stickers as fast as Dr. Wong can make them today, and I'm eating so many that I can actually feel my pants getting tighter by the minute. Not that I care. These babies are so tasty! We're all pretty focused on the food, because Liza's still annoyed that we mentioned the Totally Obvious Situation with her mom and Chef Antonio when we were texting yesterday. Apparently, we're all taking the class again (which I guess my mom would have gotten around to sharing!), and she thinks that explains everything. She says we're the ones who are clueless, but when it comes to Liza and her parents, she sort of sees what she wants to see.

During cooking class last fall, Lillian and I totally knew sparks were flying (as my dad would say) between Chef and Liza's mom. I mean, it wasn't like they were flirting up a storm or anything, but you could just tell that they liked each other by the way they talked and looked at each other. And there was that whole thing with Chef Antonio making the family recipe Liza's mom taught him. Like I said, Totally Obvious Situation, but Liza just pretended it wasn't happening. Or maybe she really couldn't see it.

I don't blame her. Who wants divorced parents? My parents have been together for an eternity. They have four kids, two jobs, a crowded house with cereal ground into the rugs and laundry literally falling from the ceiling (my brothers love the old laundry chute in our house so much that they decided to try to *dig* a second one through the floor of their room), and way too many other relatives—but they still really like each other. After eighteen years together, they still kiss when they get home from work, hold hands when they're walking, and cuddle on the couch. It's actually kind of sweet, when they're not being *too* romantic about it. (Really, guys, as my seven-year-old brother Nicky likes to say, "Not in front of the kids!")

I mean, I get it. Liza wants the kind of family she thinks she used to have, and she's not taking the Big D (that's what we call her parents' divorce) lying down. The thing is, I was around her family before her dad left, and most of the time it wasn't the way she remembers it at all. Her dad was always working, and her mom got really frustrated with all of the kid stuff and house-work she had to do, even though she has a big full-time job too. After Cole was born, they were both really happy about having another kid, but it wasn't like they became this super-tight family. I can't even remember seeing all four of them do anything together—unlike my family, who spend *way* too much time together. I think Liza's mom and dad really tried, but after a while they decided that it just wasn't working. At least that's what it looked like to me, anyway.

It's not like I can say any of this to Liza, though. As her best friend, it's my job to have her back, just like she always has mine. She just told us that she plans to use the party to undo the divorce. So if she wants to use Nana Silver's not-mitzvah as the glue to put her parents back together, then I'll be right there with her, doing the *hora* (that's a traditional Jewish dance Liza taught me after her aunt Sarah's wedding two years ago).

I grab another pot-sticker and try to pull Liza out of her funk.

"What do you guys think of this semester's new clubs?" I say. At least, that's what I mean to say, but with a mouth full of dumpling I doubt anyone can understand me.

Lillian laughs and points at my cheeks bulging with food. Of course her sister, Katie, chooses exactly this moment to appear in the kitchen. Her perfect sister. Lillian calls Katie that all the time, and honestly, she's not exaggerating. The girl is amazing. She's beautiful without looking cheesy or like she's trying too hard (or at all, really). And her clothes are so cool—"understated" is what my new favorite fashion blog would call her look—and they fit her just right, like she was the designer's muse (another piece of wisdom from the blog).

The coolest thing about Katie, though, is that she seems so confident and sure of herself. Man, I'd like to have people think that about me. Starting with my stupid brothers!

Katie sees us shoveling in our dumplings and saunters across the kitchen to grab a clementine. Dr. Wong offers her a pot-sticker, but she shakes her head.

"Too heavy for me," she says with a sniff. "I just

want a piece of fruit." As her mother makes a disapproving cluck, Katie peels her little clementine calmly and precisely, without getting all sticky from the juice. How does she do that?

Lillian is talking about something she did in art class, but my eyes are basically glued to Katie. "Do you want to sit down?" I ask her, taking my backpack off the stool next to mine. The others look at me in surprise. So does Katie.

"No, no. But thank you, Frankie. I don't have time to chat." She polishes off her snack and puts some water on to boil. "I'm going to make myself some mint tea and go upstairs. I have to write a position paper on India's independence for Model UN. We have a conference in Delaware next month. The best delegate slipped through my fingers last time," she says, wiggling her slender digits with their evenly filed, perfectly clean nails. Then she smiles. "That's not going to happen again."

Wow. Lillian isn't kidding. Katie is hardcore. But

still, she's so cool. She points to the table, littered with dumpling scraps and blobs of sauce.

"You guys quite finished, are you? I think maybe you missed a piece of cabbage."

Lillian is irritated. "We were really hungry, and these are really good."

Dr. Wong comes to our defense. "Katie, leave the girls alone. We cannot all exist on citrus and tea." Lillian's mom is an amazing cook, and she's not a pushover, either. Until very recently, I was a little afraid of her because she doesn't seem to approve of very much. But she started to actually like a few things, including cooking class after a bumpy start, so maybe she's not so scary after all.

Katie shrugs at her mother again. "No, no, no. Carbs and oil, so much better for you . . . "

Dr. Wong clicks her tongue at Katie, who stops talking immediately. Okay, so she still is a little scary. But Lillian is really getting annoyed. "Katie, nobody asked you. And don't start on your soccer-training routine again. I'm sure real athletes eat real food."

Katie pours the water into a pretty little teapot and swirls it around. "Sure, athletes eat real food— emphasis on the word 'real.' I just choose to put something in my body that's not going to weigh me down." She shrugs. "But that's just me . . ."

Really? Then why do I feel like she has a point . . . ?

Katie gives her mother a peck on the cheek as she wafts out of the room with her tea, scooping up her totally hip messenger bag on the way.

On the way home I keep thinking about Katie, sipping tea, playing soccer, and solving the world's problems at the Model UN. I have ambitions too, don't I? I played soccer in elementary school and I was pretty good. Who says I can't just transfer that talent to a spring sport, like track? I may not have gotten around to it yet, but why not start now?

Picturing myself sprinting around a track with a flawless ponytail bouncing against my back and my parents cheering from the sidelines makes me smile. Oh, and look who's behind them—none other than some cute boy, yelling out my name (hey, it's a fantasy, right?). If Katie can do it all, why couldn't I make the track team and the honor roll this semester? And give rousing speeches at seventh-grade assemblies on the need for compostable plates and cups in the cafeteria! Who says I can't be supersmart, righteous, and freakishly fast, too? Maybe I'll brew myself an elegant little cup of tea and retire to my room to plot my ambitions. Color-code a few notebooks and highlighters and index cards, just to help me juggle all the activities. *How does she do it all?* people will say—and I'll just smile modestly and wave them off. Keep calm and reshape the world to my exacting specifications. . . .

I open our front door, still thinking about the new me. When I step inside, my little brother Nicky and his friend Julian practically mow me down as they bash at each other with cardboard swords. My older brothers Leo and Joey, known as The Goons, are in the living room with a couple of other hairy teenage meatheads, trying to figure out the chords to some song on their bashed-up guitars. There's a pile of boat-size shoes right by the door. I stumble over them and practically choke from the nasty smell. Mom yells up from the basement at one brother or another—or maybe all three—and suddenly I just can't stand it. I race up the stairs and slam the door of my room. I need to get myself some *feng shui* right now!

CHAPTER 5
Liza

For the first time ever, we're not running late to cooking class on Saturday. It's a miracle. There were no tantrums, no last-minute work emergencies, no arguments. I keep looking at the curly-haired, dimpled angel in the stroller and thinking: *Who are you and what have you done with my baby brother?*

When we get there, even I'm surprised at how excited I am. Although the kitchen is all sparkling and new, everything seems really homey and comforting.

The Newlyweds—the totally adorable, totally into each other, totally just-married couple that we met in the fall session are walking in with us, oohing and ahhing about how much bigger Cole is. Mrs. Newlywed—Margo—looks really cute with a new haircut, and as usual, Mr. Newlywed—Stephen— pretty much can't take his eyes off her. They're completely googly over Cole and his chubby cheeks. He's hard to resist today, I have to admit.

When we finally make it through the door and everyone is finished drooling over Cole, Chef is all, "Welcome, welcome, *mis amigos, mis corazones.*" As we reach the long steel tables, he actually winks at us, which is cute, but kind of weird. Frankie and her mom aren't here yet, but I'm sure she and Lillian would say he's winking at my mom. Ick.

Chef's mother, Angelica, rushes over in a jangle of silver bangles to hug us all and kiss us with her red-lipsticked smile. In a snap she sweeps Cole out of the stroller and into her arms, just like she did last fall, when I was sure my brother was going to ruin an entire session of cooking classes before they'd even begun.

"*Mijo, mijo lindo,*" she sings as he dissolves into giggles. Angelica dances Cole off to their special corner, where she already has a bunch of stuff laid out for them to play with.

"Hi," I say as they spin away into their own happy world. "Nice to see you, too."

Errol and Henry, the two old college friends who are probably now in their fifties (older than our parents, that much I can tell) and planning to open a restaurant together, are already sitting at one of the tables. Except, wait a minute, someone else is sitting with them too—a cute boy with blondish skateboarder hair and dark gray eyes. Not really my type, but definitely noticeable. I try to get a better look at him without flat-out staring, while Errol wraps Mom and me in big warm hugs.

"Hey, gorgeous girls," Errol says. "Aren't you both a sight for sore eyes!" He's from the south like my mom and has one of those smiles that people describe as "infectious." I mean, it always makes *me* feel better, I know that.

He points to the cute skater kid. "I want you all to meet my nephew, Tristan Holland."

"Hey," Tristan says, with a sort of half wave. Not a chatty guy, I'm guessing.

While Henry asks Chef all about the new kitchen design, Errol tells Mom and me that he was inspired by our mother-daughter togetherness last session. He thought taking a cooking class would be a great way to spend some time with his nephew, now that he's in ninth grade and not so big on field trips to the zoo. It doesn't look to me like Tristan is so into this idea either—it actually looks like he'd rather be anywhere else—but Errol is so pumped about it that I hope it works.

I feel a tap on my shoulder and manage to tear myself away from staring at Tristan long enough to turn around.

"Hi, Liza," Lillian says, smiling like a jack-o'-lantern. "Fancy meeting you here."

Lillian and I hug like we haven't seen each other in months, even though it's actually been less than twenty-four hours. Over her shoulder I see Dr. Wong, who's busy inspecting the appliances in that very serious, scientific way of hers. One of the cake mixers gets a nod—she must be impressed.

Lillian and I are still hugging when the studio door slams open and everyone spins around to see who it is. In their typical Caputo family frenzy, Frankie and her mom rush in, late to class as usual. Despite the fact that there's an incredibly cute boy just a few feet away, Lillian and I grab each other's hands and jump up and down like total goofballs— we're all here! Oh well, he's bound to see us act like dorks eventually. Frankie waves excitedly at us, and then her eyes go wide like an anime cartoon, and I can tell they've landed on Tristan. Frankie has some special radar that's super sensitive to any hot boys in the area. Uh-oh. All the way from across the room, I can hear the gears cranking in her head.

Frankie's mom, Theresa, hugs mine, and—to my surprise—the very proper, a little bit scary, Dr. Wong. I guess everyone is excited to be here.

Chef Antonio claps his hands. "Okay, good people! We are all back together again, *mis amigos*, so let's get cooking! We shall roll up our sleeves and dust the hands and make some tasty pastries!" Sometimes Chef really reminds me of a thinner Cuban Santa Claus, he's that jolly.

When Chef gets started, it's hard not to get caught up in his mood. Today we're tackling cookies, he says, since no one can resist a cookie. Apparently, on the food history time line, crackers came before cookies, and some kind of crackerlike item has been around forever. Basically, they're just flour and water made into a paste with salt or spices to preserve them. When you break it down like that, it doesn't sound so yummy to me, but

I guess that's all a Saltine is, and there's nothing better when you're sick.

Chef tells us how crackers used to be baked twice to keep them firm, which is where the French word *biscuit*, or "twice cooked," came from. Eventually people started adding sugar, spices, and fruit to make the sweet biscuits we call cookies today. So where did we get the word "cookie," you might ask yourself. Good question! And, of course, Chef has an answer: The Dutch called them *koekje* when they came to this country, and since Americans were pretty anti-everything-British for a while, they decided to use the Dutch word, which morphed into "cookie."

"So, everybody, step up to the tables and let's bake some cookies!" Chef Antonio hollers after our history lesson.

Frankie gives me a look like, "Here we go again," as she and her disaster-in-the-kitchen mom take their places at one of the long work tables covered with little bowls of flour, sugar, and other ingredients.

Lillian and Dr. Wong stay with Errol and his nephew at one table, so Henry joins the smiling, snuggling Newlyweds. That leaves Mom and me together, until Chef appears. So he's helping us, I guess? I can think of other people who need it more . . .

Chef tells us all to start with the softened butter, which needs to be creamed, first by itself and then with the sugar. We crack the eggs—I hear Theresa, Frankie's mom, shriek when an egg rolls out of her hand and off the table with a splat. "Here we go again" is right. I don't even need to look at Frankie—I can feel her embarrassment all the way over here.

We sift flour, baking soda, and salt and mix it all up. The first thing we're making is some dough that needs to chill in the fridge before we can shape it. As we follow the recipes propped up on clear plastic clipboards, Chef brings some tables melted chocolate to fold into the dough. Some of us will be making chocolate logs, while the others will make vanilla ones. Luckily, Mom and I are at a chocolate table.

Later, when we slice our logs into cookies that are round and flat, we get to put all sorts of toppings on them. So that explains all the little bowls of nuts, dried fruit, and candies. Yum.

We shape the dough with our hands and then roll it into a log. It's fun to do and I think I'm doing a pretty good job with mine, while Mom and Chef bond over the fact that growing up, both of their mothers called refrigerators "ice boxes" (I'm guessing Angelica's version was in Spanish—I know "ice" is *hielo*, but I don't think I've ever learned the word for "box"—I make a mental note to ask Javier, if he ever shows up). We all carry our rolls over to chill for a few minutes in the freezer, and I notice both Lillian and Frankie (maybe Tristan too, but it's hard to tell) giggling at the chocolate logs on our tray. Are they less impressive than I thought? I take another look and realize that the little brown rolls do sort of look like rows of, well . . . there's no other way to say it, *turds*. I laugh along because it is kind of funny in a gross way, but part of me wishes I'd never made the connection between my edible creations and well, you know what. Whatever. I'm sure they'll taste better than that. And anyway, Frankie's mom's rolls look more like lumpy snakes that are busy digesting a bunch of rats than a soon-to-be tray of cookies, so we all end up laughing at them, too.

Frankie, Lillian, and I are still cracking up when Javier strolls in through a door in the back of the studio, where Chef Antonio has his office. He looks around like he's just landed in the Emerald City. "Whoa, I forgot this was starting up again today," he says, making a big show of surprise and running his hand through his dark, shiny curls. Hardly. He totally knew we were coming—we've been texting him about it all week. I guess he thinks pretending he has more important things to do than keep track of our cooking-class schedule makes him seem cool, or mysterious.

Javier turns to Frankie, Lillian, and me. "Hey guys," he starts to say—and then he notices Tristan.

All of a sudden, it's like when Frankie's pug Rocco smells a cat—or maybe more like another dog. Javi looks Tristan up and down like he's trying to decide if he's someone he wants to be friends with, or avoid.

"Dude," Javier mutters, tipping his chin up in some weird boy greeting.

"Dude," Tristan says back. End of discussion.

I roll my eyes at Frankie, who shakes her head in agreement. Boys. Lillian, on the other hand, can't seem to take her eyes off Javier, even though now that his riveting conversation with Tristan is over, he doesn't seem to know what to do with himself. This session of cooking class is definitely getting interesting. . . .

While the rolls are firming up so we can slice them, we make *biscotti*—Italian cookies. More dough ingredients, except that this time, we use olive oil instead of butter. We get to toss any of the goodies from the little bowls on the table into the biscotti—

cranberries, pistachios, almonds, slivered ginger—anything that we want. . . . I like coming up with wacky combinations—chocolate and dried blueberries! cinnamon and candied orange peel!—and mixing them into the dough. Since this dough is a little stickier than the one we made for the logs, we have to dip our hands in water to shape it into rectangles, which feels kind of slimy.

I guess seeing all of our disgusted faces makes Javi want to join, so he dunks his hands into the water on Frankie's table. Since he doesn't have any dough (duh!), he decides to fling the water off his hands instead—in Tristan's direction. Maybe it was on purpose, maybe not, it's hard to say—but Javier is definitely not into the fact that there's some competition for him in the class this time around. Luckily, Errol saves the day.

"Javier," he says, waving Javi over, "I'd like you to meet my nephew Tristan. He was a little concerned about being the only boy with all of these lovely young ladies, so I'm sure he'd be really thrilled if you'd stick around."

Clearly embarrassed, Tristan gives Errol the evil eye, but Errol just smiles and hands him a paper towel to wipe off his still-wet face. Tristan's not really my type (do I even have a type?), but blushing somehow makes him even cuter. Frankie's practically drooling.

I guess what Errol said worked, because Javier— whose surly-puppy face has suddenly morphed into his I'm-the-man look—strolls over to Tristan and holds out his hand, palm up.

"Sorry, man," he says, nodding his head toward Frankie. "I was aiming for her."

Frankie half laughs, half snorts at Javi—yeah right, nice try—but he ignores her.

Tristan smiles. "S'okay," he says, slapping Javi's hand. A high five? Really? Boys don't make any sense.

Chef sends Javi to the sink to wash his hands and claps at the rest of us again. "Now we will make some very special chocolate chip cookies. You can do this anytime, if you have the leftover Easter bunnies or Valentine's hearts or just want to make bigger chocolate pieces!"

Instead of using regular chocolate chips, we get to cut up these really fancy chocolate bars into different size pieces. I look over at Lillian's table and notice that her mom is actually letting her cut them—but of course she's making sure that every piece is as perfect and even as possible. Mom's and mine look pretty good, although there are chocolate shavings all over. Chef doesn't seem to mind, though—is it my imagination or is he coming by every few minutes to brush off our table?

After we mix our chocolate chunks into yet another bowl of dough, we drop spoonfuls onto baking sheets to go into the huge, gleaming ovens.

"These very special cookies will emerge in a few minutes, so, okay, *mis amigos*, while those are becoming golden brown morsels of deliciousness, how about we slice some logs?"

While most of us cut the logs into little round cookies, Frankie and Lillian get to make icing that will get pressed between some of them as sandwich cookies. At our table Mom and I make a thumbprint on each cookie and then press a nut or an M&M into it for decoration. Meanwhile, we're also working on the biscotti, which we'll bake once, take out, slice into strips, and then put back in the oven so they're hard enough for dunking in coffee or hot chocolate.

Just as the biscotti are going into the oven for the second time, Chef announces that we're going to cram one more recipe in—meringues—even though we're running out of time. He has already prepared bowls of egg whites that he tells us to whip into "stiff peaks" with the giant professional mixers.

"Make mountain tops, *señors y señoritas*, mountain tops! But first, while the egg white is still foamy like the tip of an ocean wave, sprinkle more *dulces* from the little bowls—chocolate, fruit, nuts—anything is good baked in little meringue."

Over the noise of the mixers, Chef tells us about all the shapes meringue can take—flowers or cups or nests. My mom starts squealing—seriously—about how we could make these for my birthday party and fill them with ice cream. Ugh. I was having such a good time and totally *not* thinking about the dreaded birthday party—why did she have to bring it up?

Luckily, everybody seems too busy with the last-minute meringues or twice-baking their biscotti or not burning the other cookies to even really notice. Lillian and Frankie are both arguing with their moms—Dr. Wong won't let Lillian "operate heavy machinery" like the mixer, and the Caputos just can't get their egg whites to peak. I'm not big on conflict, but right now I'm glad they're all too preoccupied to join in my mom's birthday party menu planning.

It really is good to be back!

CHAPTER 6
Liza

Now that second semester has started, seventh-graders are allowed to eat lunch in the quad, along with the eighth-graders who have had it to themselves since September. So far it's been too cold to eat outside, but today is one of those weirdly warm January days when all you need is a fall jacket, and maybe a scarf if your mom gives you a hard time (which, of course, mine does). Frankie, Lillian, and I have staked out a corner of the quad, and we're sitting cross-legged on our coats with our lunches lined up in the middle like a mini buffet. The sky is practically cloudless, and the sun feels so good on our faces that we all close our eyes for a minute and soak it in, like we're plants desperate to photosynthesize after a long winter.

The sun is so warm on my skin that I almost feel like I'm still at my dad's in California. Unfortunately, thinking about LA reminds me of the party, and an icy wave crashes through my toasty daydream. I open my eyes.

Frankie's poking through the couscous salad I brought, picking out the raisins and piling them up in one corner of the container. She has a thing about raisins in savory food because she thinks they don't match the other flavors. Frankie has been acting kind of quiet and distracted, which isn't unusual on days that we have social studies right after lunch. I'm about to tease her about still having a crush on Mr. Mac, when Lillian yanks her backpack open and pulls out a bulging plastic bag.

"I forgot I brought these!" she says, adding what's left of the cookies she and her mom took home from Saturday's cooking class to our smorgasbord.

Frankie pauses her archeological exploration of the couscous and looks up at us. "You know Errol's nephew—what's his name—he was sitting at my table?"

She asks this in an overly casual way, but she's not fooling anyone. Frankie pretending she doesn't remember a cute boy's name can mean only one thing. I raise my eyebrows at Lillian.

"You mean *Tristan*?" Lillian says, unzipping the bag of cookies.

"Oh, right, that was it," Frankie says, still acting cool as a cucumber. "So, he seems kind of nice, right? Taking a cooking class with his uncle and everything."

Lillian pulls a perfect-looking meringue out of the bag. "He didn't say a whole lot," she says, taking a bite and starting to giggle, "but he was totally hot!"

Lillian always giggles when she talks about boys, which cracks me up.

"Tristan Holland," I say, "a.k.a. Total Hotness. But a ninth grader. I don't know, Franks, isn't that like cradle robbing for you, after liking Mr. Mac all this time?"

Lillian laughs again, sending little pieces of meringue flying out of her mouth. She quickly covers it with her hand.

Frankie puts down her fork, glaring at me. "Ha-ha. Whatever. I guess he was pretty cute," she shrugs. "You guys don't, like, *like* him or anything . . . do you?"

I roll my eyes. The truth is, I've been so busy thinking about the party and the whole thing with my mom and dad that there isn't any room in my brain for boys right now. "No," I say. "But I know who does."

"Who?" Frankie asks, dropping her casual act and sounding concerned.

I give her shoulder a shove. "You do, you faker! It's so obvious."

Frankie blushes. "I so do not! No way. I hardly even know him."

"Well, you have six weeks to get to know him," Lillian says. "We'll have to figure out a way to make sure he's in your group on Saturday."

"I know! I was thinking the same thing," Frankie says, giving up her pretense and grabbing our hands. "You guys have to help me." The force of her grip crushes the cookie I'm holding, and the crumbs fall onto the remains of Lillian's sesame noodles like sprinkles on a sundae. Frankie lets go. "Okay, maybe I do like him a little."

"Uh, yeah," I say, brushing biscotti crumbs off my jacket and hoping it's still too cold for ants.

"Well, if I do, I'm not the only one with a cooking class crush," Frankie says, giving Lillian the one-raised-eyebrow treatment.

Lillian turns as red as the marinara sauce on Frankie's pasta. Even though she hasn't told us, Frankie and I can tell Lillian likes Javier by the way she looks at him when she thinks he doesn't see her, and how she gets extra quiet when he's around.

Frankie's eyes light up. "Guys, I have a totally brilliant idea."

I check my phone. "Does it have to do with teleporting to Mr. Mac's class?" I ask. "Because if we don't get going soon we'll be late."

"No," Frankie says, as we all start cleaning up. "It has to do with your birthday party."

"Ugh. Did you have to mention the not-mitzvah?"

"Yes, I did," says Frankie, dumping what's left of her half-eaten pasta into a trash can, "because the party is the perfect opportunity for me and Lillian to get to know a certain pair of boys a little—or maybe even a lot—better!"

Lillian drops the bag of cookies she was about to shove into her backpack. "What? Frankie, do you lie awake at night thinking up evil boy-related plans?"

Yes, probably, I think.

"Calm down, Lils, I'm not talking about doing anything creepy or stalkerish," Frankie says, picking up the broken cookies. "I'm not even suggesting that we ask them to the party *ourselves*. Nana Silver's going to do it for us—from Liza, I mean. What do you think, Lize?"

"Guys, I'm sure they'll be on the list," I say. "I mean, I don't really know Tristan, but he's Errol's nephew and I'm planning to invite the whole class."

Frankie looks pleased with herself. Lillian looks ill.

Lucky for Lillian, the two-minute warning bell rings, and the three of us make a mad rush for the door along with everyone else who decided to have lunch in the quad. As I'm absorbed into the mob of middle school bodies, I replay our conversation in my head. Suddenly the party that I wish I'd never agreed to has become an event my two best friends are looking forward to (or at least one of them, anyway). This probably sounds selfish, but I realize that I don't want Frankie and Lillian to be excited about my party—I want them to totally dread it, just like me!

CHAPTER 7
Lillian

Now that we've been taking cooking class together, every once in a while my mother lets me help out in the kitchen at home. Tonight is one of those rare occasions: she's making a shrimp dish, and it's my job to peel them. I'm not going to lie, peeling shrimp isn't exactly my favorite kitchen chore, but there is actually some skill involved, so my mother asking me to do it is kind of a big deal.

The shrimp peeler is really sharp, and slicing

open the shell while also removing the vein along the shrimp's back takes practice (I know that sounds totally gross, but it's really not that bad once you get used to it). The trick is to do it quickly, without cutting off your finger in the process. Having to be rushed off to the emergency room for a kitchen accident would definitely not increase my mother's confidence in my skills. Luckily, she bought enough shrimp to feed the whole block, so I'll have plenty of time to perfect my technique.

I'm just getting into a good peeling rhythm when Katie comes in the back door. She's been out running, and there are damp spots darkening her tank top under her arms. Even sweaty, she's practically flawless. Her cheeks are flushed and her ponytail is still perky. If it wasn't for a few flyaway hairs and the faint sweat stains, you might think she'd just stepped out to the corner deli to buy the bottle of water she's chugging, rather than run two three-mile loops around Prospect Park—the biggest park in Brooklyn.

Katie puts the bottle down, takes a deep breath, and then scrunches up her face.

"Ew," she says, pinching her nose, "what exactly is that smell?"

I hold up a drippy handful of peeled (and deveined!) shrimp and give her an extra perky grin. "Dinner."

"Really, Lillian, that's just disgusting," Katie says, holding up her hand to block her view and turning away. "Are you trying to make me throw up?"

"That is *enough*, WeiWei," my mother says firmly. "I do not put 'disgusting' food on my table." For a girl whose Chinese name means "mighty" and "powerful," Katie is acting pretty wimpy about a pile of raw seafood.

I go back to peeling shrimp, making sure to hold each one high enough so that Katie can't avoid seeing me slice the shell along its back. "And didn't you get straight As in biology last year?" I ask. "How is what I'm doing any more gross than dissecting a frog or a scorpion?"

I fully expect my mother to snap at me for egging Katie on, but she looks up just long enough to give me one of her "warning stares" and goes back to chopping bok choy. She's a biology professor, so maybe she agrees.

Katie glares at me and then turns to my mother. "I'll just have some steamed vegetables tonight, Mama," she says. "With a small scoop of brown rice."

"I bought two pounds of shrimp at the fish market," my mother says, her knife moving rhythmically along the thick white stems. "*Jiāo yán xiā* has always been one of your favorite dishes."

Jiāo yán xiā is salt-and-pepper shrimp. It's one of the foods that Chinese people traditionally serve on Lunar New Year, but my mother's is so tasty that we all beg her to make it year-round. Or at least we all used to.

Katie tosses her water bottle into the recycling bin. "Shrimp is full of cholesterol. I can't put that in my body while I'm in training." She squeezes past my mother and heads for the table where her backpack is slung over the back of a chair.

Mama waves her hand dismissively. "I am not running a restaurant," she says, pointing to the rice cooker. "We are having white rice tonight."

Katie takes a massive textbook out of her bag and shrugs. "I guess I'll just have greens, then." She holds up the giant book, which I now see is a Shakespeare anthology. My sister is in the advanced English literature class, of course. "I'm off to memorize my sonnet in the bath. We're reciting them tomorrow, and Mr. Gupta says I have a 'flare for the Bard,' so I don't want to disappoint him."

I've heard Shakespeare called "the Bard" before, but who even knows what that means? Katie does, of course, like she knows everything. Or like she thinks she knows everything. She's only fifteen, but she acts like she's in college. I don't know how her friends can stand it. Not that she's made any real friends since we moved to Brooklyn anyway. There were a couple of girls on her soccer team who came over a few times back in the fall, and she texts sometimes with her Model UN teammates, but she's always so busy studying or working out or preparing for a competition, I don't know when she'd have time for friends even if she wanted them.

I finish peeling the last of the shrimp and remind myself how lucky I am to have made friends like Liza and Frankie. I don't even like to think about those first few weeks of school before Mr. Mac put me in their project group and Liza came up with her Big Idea to take Chef Antonio's cooking class. Moving clear across the country and having to leave my cousin Chloe and my best friend Sierra behind in San Francisco was the worst. I've never felt as lonely as I did that first day at Clinton Middle School, standing in the cafeteria and not seeing a single friendly face at any of the tables.

Maybe Katie would be nicer if she had some real friends too. Even back in San Francisco she spent more time with all of her clubs and teams than with any of the girls on our block or in her class. When we were little, our parents made us go to Chinese school every Saturday—all day. I don't know how I would have survived if Chloe and I weren't always in the same class (our birthdays are so close, we call ourselves "twin cousins"). I would have died of boredom without someone to pass notes to, or to make fun of the teacher with behind her back. But Katie didn't have anyone like Chloe to get her through Chinese school every week. She was as serious about getting straight As there as she was in regular school—the other kids were probably afraid to even talk to her.

My mother finishes chopping the bok choy and scoops all of the pieces into a colander for rinsing. Holding it under the water with one hand, she reaches into a cabinet with the other and pulls out a small bamboo steamer. She puts a handful of bok choy into the steamer, replaces the lid, and pushes it aside with a sigh. "Your stubborn sister can steam them herself," she says.

I wonder if she knows that "stubborn" is exactly how most people would describe her, too.

CHAPTER 8
Liza

Nana Silver is taking me to see some "venues" after school today. She called this morning all excited to tell me that she's been "scouring the city" for the perfect place to have my party, and she's narrowed down her list to a few "real gems" that she can't wait to show me. Spending a whole afternoon looking at party rooms isn't exactly my idea of a good time, but if I let my Nana choose the place without checking it out myself, I guarantee she'll pick the one that looks the most like the royal ballroom in Cinderella.

A couple of years ago Nana decided she was "too old to take the subway" anymore, so she takes taxis wherever she goes (never mind that my science teacher, Mr. Stubbs—I know, unfortunate name— is older than she is, and he rides his bike to school every day). Since we'll be making a bunch of stops today, though, she actually hired a car and driver for the entire afternoon. While we're looking at "venues," the car will be waiting for us outside. When I texted Frankie to tell her, she texted back, *SO COOL! I'm jelly!* But to me the whole thing is totally embarrassing—like we think we're so fancy with a chauffeur-driven limo.

"Here," Nana says when I complain about the car. She hands me a pair of seriously oversize sunglasses. "Put these on and nobody will recognize you."

The sunglasses could not be more Nana's style and less mine, but I put them on anyway and check my reflection in the window. I look ridiculous.

Nana nudges my shoulder. "See, darling?" she smiles. "Problem solved."

If only. I take a selfie wearing the insane glasses and send it to Frankie and Lillian. I'm sure they'll find my misery as amusing as Nana Silver does.

Our first stop is surprisingly less glitzy than I expected. It's a big loft space in a very cool, very expensive neighborhood called DUMBO (which stands for Down Under the Manhattan Bridge Overpass and has nothing to do with the Disney elephant). Back in the 1970s, the neighborhood was full of industrial lofts that artists took over. Pretty soon, DUMBO became a hot place to live, with cool restaurants, art galleries, and all that. These days it's way too expensive for artists or anyone who doesn't make a gazillion dollars a year. But it's still a nice neighborhood to walk around, and there's a really great park along the waterfront with my favorite ice cream place and amazing views of the bridges and the Manhattan skyline.

The loft is big and white and very bright, with giant windows taking up most of three of the walls. Talk about views! I bet it's incredible at night when all the lights are on along the bridges and in the office buildings across the river. Renting this place for a night probably costs more than our apartment does for a whole month, but it's on Nana's list, so she must be able to afford it. And if she insists on throwing me a party, I think this "venue" will do just fine.

Unfortunately, Nana and I aren't exactly "on the same page" as my mom used to say about herself and my dad. "This is the plainest of all the rooms I'm going to show you," she says. "It's big, but it's nothing special."

"But what about the view at night? It must be incredible," I say, pointing to the Brooklyn Bridge out one window and the Manhattan Bridge out another.

"The views are nice," Nana says with a shrug, "but if everyone's looking out the windows, nobody will be looking at you!"

Exactly! "That's okay, Nana. I don't want everyone to be looking at me."

"Nonsense," she says, waving me off. "It's your special day. You should feel like a princess!"

Ugh. This afternoon is definitely starting to go as expected. I text Nana's princess line to Frankie and Lillian. Frankie sends me back a crown emoji surrounded by little hearts. *Not* helpful.

The next place we visit is a little fancier than the loft, but it's not completely obnoxious. It's a big room in the back of an Italian restaurant that I've heard people talk about on some of my cooking shows, but I've never been there. The walls are mostly mirrored and there's a painting on the ceiling, but there's no gold paint or chandeliers. It's not exactly my style, but I could live with it.

It is not a shock to me that (even though this place is on her list!) Nana looks totally less than thrilled. She's just come back from talking to the manager, and she's shaking her head. "You can't have outside catering," she says. "All of the food has to be provided by the restaurant."

That makes sense to me—what restaurant would want people bringing in food from someplace else for a party? "That's okay with me," I shrug, trying to show how accommodating I am, "I love Italian food."

"That's nice," says Nana, "but you won't love having tomato sauce stains all over your pretty dress. Red sauce and party clothes do not go together."

"Can't we just bring extra napkins?"

Nana shakes her head, tugging one of my braids. "Cute," she says, even though I wasn't trying to be.

We see three more places—all in Manhattan—each with a little more flash than the one before. The last one might as well be Buckingham Palace. Nana is in heaven.

"Don't you love it, Liza?" she says, opening her arms to emphasize the glittering expanse of the room.

I take a long hard look at her to make sure she's not actually holding a wand.

"It's pretty," I say, trying to start off on a positive note, "but it's, uh, a little too fancy, don't you think?"

Nana pretends to look surprised. "Not at all, darling, not at all. It's perfect." She straightens a fold on one of the long velvet curtains. "And besides, we can always tone it down."

I try not to panic, and force myself to smile. "Even if we could, Nana, it's in Manhattan. All of my friends live in Brooklyn, and most of Mom's, too."

My grandmother puts her arm around my shoulders. "But my friends are all in Manhattan, sweetheart, and it's harder for people my age to get around the city. You understand that, right?"

This from the woman with a car and driver waiting at the curb. I could remind her, but there's no point. Instead, I wander around the room while she stands there beaming. I must be looking pouty, because finally she throws up her hands.

"I can see this isn't your favorite," Nana says. "That's okay, that's why I brought you along. It's your party, after all."

Is it? You could have fooled me.

"So you're not going to rent out this place?" I ask, hopefully.

"I still have to do some price comparisons and look into a few other details. But your lack of enthusiasm about this venue is duly noted."

Nana's nonanswer isn't totally reassuring, and her chilly tone is intended to make me feel bad, but I'm a little bit relieved anyway. At least this is the last "venue" of the day. I snap a photo of the Buckingham ballroom while Nana isn't looking and send it to Frankie and Lillian. *Gotta go*, I type. *My carriage awaits.*

Outside by the car Nana says she's staying in Manhattan and will get a cab home. She tells the driver to take me back to Brooklyn. "And don't try anything funny," she warns him, giving him a distinctive Nana

Silver glare. "That's my granddaughter and I know what you look like and where you work." She makes a show of studying his ID posted on the dashboard and takes a picture with her phone.

I slink down into my seat. Nana's protectiveness is sweet, I guess, but I feel terrible for the driver, who has been extremely professional and perfectly nice to us all day.

"Sorry," I say as we pull into traffic.

The driver (whose name is Vikas, according to the card I've read at least a hundred times) laughs. "No worries," he says. "You are lucky to have a grandmother who cares only for your happiness."

Now it's my turn to laugh. *Ha!* I think. *My happiness? If you only knew.*

CHAPTER 9
Liza

"This Spanish assignment is giving me a stomach-ache," Lillian says. We're over at Frankie's doing our homework in the kitchen, which is the only room that is temporarily free of her brothers and assorted random boys throughout the house. Her dad is not on duty today, so he's apparently doing little repairs all over the place—tightening hinges on doors, patching small holes in plaster, changing a shower head. The Caputos' house takes a beating, I guess, because

Frankie's dad is always doing this kind of thing—when he's not in the kitchen cooking, I mean.

"You're probably just hungry," I tell Lillian. "Check out the cabinet next to the microwave—it's where the Caputos keep their snacks."

"Is that okay, Frankie?" Lillian asks. Sometimes I forget that she hasn't grown up in our houses the way Frankie and I have in each other's.

"Huh?" Frankie looks up at the sound of her name. For some reason she's been pouring over the "Spring Clubs and Teams" flyer Ms. Hirshman handed out in advisory today. "Oh, sure. Yeah, take whatever you want."

Lillian opens the snack cabinet and practically has a stroke. "Oh my God, Liza—look at all this food!"

I've seen the contents of the snack cabinet a thousand times, but it's not something you ever get used to. There's a shelf full of chips of every kind—potato, tortilla, barbecue, salt and vinegar, veggie sticks, you name it, if it's salty and crunches, it's there—and another that's crammed with cookies. The rest of the shelves are stocked with cereal, crackers, granola bars, "healthy" Pop-Tarts, and pretty much anything else that exists to satisfy the munchies. The crazy thing is, between Frankie and her brothers (especially her brothers) and all of their friends, the Caputos can easily clean out the entire cabinet in a week. Frankie's dad must have gone grocery shopping this morning.

"I know—it's like a dream come true," I say, thinking of the pathetically empty shelves in our kitchen. When we have snacks around, my mother goes for healthy, organic stuff because of Cole. But sometimes you need junk food . . . "So what are we having?"

I recognize Lillian's stunned expression as she stares into the cabinet: snack sensory overload. "I have no idea," she says. "I want it all. My parents probably don't even know the snack aisle in the supermarket exists."

Frankie puts down the flyer and looks at Lillian

and the overflowing snack closet. "Yeah, we have a ton of it. My brothers eat round the clock, but I am not that into that stuff. You guys can have whatever, though."

Lillian and I exchange a look. We may really like good food, but we're definitely not against snack food too. At least, we never used to be.

"Come on, Frankie, you love cheese curls. And you made nachos in Señora Valentin's microwave for lunch last week."

"I think you've been spending too much time at my house," says Lillian, reaching for the family-size box of microwave popcorn packets. "You're starting to sound like Katie."

"No I'm not," Frankie says, her cheeks turning pink. "I'm just tired of living with a bunch of pigs." She gets up and opens the cabinet above the sink.

"Wow—you guys have so much pasta!" Lillian says, her eyes practically popping out like an anime cartoon. "And so many different kinds!"

Full-on blushing now, Frankie slams the door shut and shoves a jar at Lillian. "Hey, Lillian, let's make this instead."

Lillian takes the jar, which is full of dried corn kernels, and looks skeptically at Frankie. "But why? Microwave popcorn is so much easier."

"And so much tastier," I add. "Do you even know how to make the other kind?"

"Of course I do," Frankie says (she's not big on admitting she doesn't know how to do things). She opens a cabinet full of appliances and reaches way into the back, shoving aside an endless supply of blenders, pasta makers, food processors, and who knows what else. After loud crashing and serious tugging, she finally digs out an ancient air-popper and slams it down on the counter. "Ta-da!"

"Was that one of your parents' wedding presents?" I ask.

"Engagement, actually," Frankie says, blowing some dust off the lid. "But it still works—we used it in December to make popcorn garlands for our Christmas tree."

I look at Lillian, hoping she'll keep pushing the microwave popcorn. Instead she hands the jar back to Frankie and shrugs. Lillian is not big on conflict.

"Fine," I say, opening the fridge. "Anything is edible when it's smothered in butter."

Frankie pours the kernels into the machine and turns it on. "I bet it's good without butter too," she says. Clearly, someone has kidnapped my oldest friend and replaced her with a health-food alien.

Luckily for us—but not for the Caputos' air popper—we don't have to find out. As the popper heats up, the part that holds the kernels starts to smoke. "Here it comes," Frankie says, but nothing pops. A few sparks fly into the shoot where the popcorn is supposed to come pouring out, and the air smells like melting plastic. Lillian yanks the plug out of the wall and opens a window. We definitely don't need Mr. Caputo's crew from the firehouse coming down to rescue us from an exploding popcorn maker.

I pick up the box of microwave popcorn. "Can we make this kind now, Franks?"

"Fine," Frankie sighs. "Whatever."

I heat up a bag of popcorn and Lillian takes a big bowl out of the dish rack. We watch the bag magically expand as the kernels pop, and when the timer goes off I pull the top open extra carefully to avoid getting a face full of steam. The salty-buttery-popcorn-y smell is amazing.

"Yum," says Lillian, grabbing a handful even before I've finished pouring it into the bowl.

I shake the last few kernels left in the bag directly into my mouth. "Sooo yummy."

Frankie takes a deep breath. "I'm full just from the smell. You guys can split it."

"You really do sound like Katie," I say. "No offense, Lillian."

"I wish I had a sister like Katie," Frankie says,

narrowing her eyes at Nicky and his friends, who are screaming fart jokes at each other in the backyard. "She's so smart and mature. And gorgeous. And, I don't know . . . confident."

"And stuck up and mean," Lillian says, scooping up more popcorn. "Trust me, you wouldn't want to live with her."

"I'd trade my disgusting brothers for her in a minute," Frankie says, slamming the window shut. "If I hear Nicky say the word 'butt' one more time I'm going to strangle him."

I decide it's time to change the subject and pick up the "Spring Clubs and Teams" flyer Frankie had been reading. The list is pretty much the usual: softball, baseball, track, French club, service club, debate team . . . "Is there anything good on here, Franks? You were studying it like there's going to be a quiz."

"I don't know," Frankie says with a shrug. "Maybe." She turns to Lillian. "Your sister runs track in the spring, right?"

Lillian rolls her eyes. "Uh-huh. And swimming in the winter, and soccer in the fall . . ."

I reach for the popcorn bowl, which is already half empty. "Why do you care, Frankie? Aren't you always ranting about The Goons being dumb jocks?"

"Those two are total dimwits," Frankie says, "but I never said *all* athletes were dumb. Katie's a major genius, isn't she?"

Lillian shoves the bowl of popcorn toward Frankie. "You know what's genius? This popcorn. Have some, Frankie. Please!"

Frankie stares at the popcorn for a few seconds, and then lets out a big sigh. "Okay, fine. I can't stand it anymore. The smell is just too amazing." She grabs a handful and shovels it into her mouth. "*Mmmm*, so good," Frankie says, little pieces of corn flying everywhere. To my relief, she actually reaches for another flat, pancaked bag and throws it into the microwave to fluff. "We are definitely going to need more of this!"

CHAPTER 10
Liza

We battle our way to cooking class in the midst of what they call a nor'easter. I'm not sure what atmospheric forces are smashing into each other to create this storm, but it's nasty. Cold, sideways-shooting rain, inside-out umbrellas, major winds, and absolutely no way to see even right in front of you as you slosh toward your destination. When I looked out the window this morning, I seriously thought about asking my mom if we could skip Chef Antonio's class this week, but then I remembered how toasty and welcoming it would be when we got there.

And I'm sure it will be, just as soon as I stop dripping all over everything, and we've un-mummified Cole from his slippery layers of rain gear. It looks like everyone else is just as soaked as we are—there are puddles all over the shiny floor, and when Frankie comes in, her thick hair is drenched and totally matted against her head. She's so pretty that it doesn't matter, but I see her trying to dry and fluff it out, looking nervously over at Tristan who is talking to Errol and Henry. They look damp, too, but somehow Tristan manages to maintain his cuteness. Frankie notices this bonus feature of Tristan's too—I can tell.

Of course, Chef, Angelica, and Javier are totally dry and perky as ever (well, Chef and Angelica, anyway). Even though I know they don't live in the studio, it sort of seems like their natural habitat. Chef is throwing thick red towels all over the floor and handing one to each of us as we walk in. My mom is particularly soaked, because she couldn't hold an umbrella and push Cole's stroller at the same time, and Chef sort of ruffles her hair as she attempts to dry it. I have to admit, it's kind of a weird move, but I decide to ignore it—and Lillian, who I catch giving Frankie a look. They're just trying to make a big deal out of nothing. When Chef does nice things for their moms, they don't call it flirting.

When we're as dry as we're going to get for the moment, Angelica whisks off my soggy brother to another part of the studio to dance around and sing their Spanish songs. Chef tosses the last of the soggy towels in a big basket and does his clapping thing to get our attention.

"*Amigos!* Here we are. *Un poco húmeda*—a little bit damp—but we are all together, cozy and warm. Has there ever been a better day to bake some comforting pies?"

He looks around the room, trying to pump us all up. The Newlyweds do seem psyched, but then again, they always do. And Errol and Henry are nodding. The rest of us aren't quite dry and ready enough to get too excited just yet. But Chef keeps going.

"Pies are *fantástico*, no? Such clever little pockets. They were created by very smart people long ago—as far back as the Greeks. Crust, *mis amigos*, was like the container, or the basket, for the filling, which could be anything they had, anything they needed to use or store or preserve for their journeys. I don't want to freak anybody out, as my son likes to say" (one look over at Javi and I can see that he's super embarrassed. Lillian notices too—I think she might even be blushing for him), "but pies were actually called little 'coffins' because they were like pastry boxes to hold meat and other food before it spoiled!"

Tristan makes a face. Clearly he's not used to Chef's . . . unique . . . sense of humor yet.

"But don't worry!" Chef Antonio assures us, catching Tristan's eye. "Our pies will be bursting with life. *Yo prometo*—I promise. No coffins in this cooking studio!"

I imagine myself back in ancient Greece, jostling along on horseback, reaching for my little pastry coffin . . . No wonder Chef has such a great show, he definitely knows how to "paint a picture with his words" as my English teacher Ms. Bissessar always says.

"So, *señoras, señoritas, y señors*, we are going to have some fun today. I want to shake things up a little, so bear with me, *por favor*. So many people are scared of pie crust, there is so much anxiety about making it. Never fear! I will help you make a flaky and tasty crust, but it cannot be hurried. And I want us to make lots of delicious options so we can all experience *las vastas* possibilities pies offer!

Chef Antonio pauses, like an actor in a play, giving us a minute to fully absorb his deep excitement over pie making. I look over at my mom, who's smiling at Chef the way she does at Cole when he does something particularly adorable. I have to admit that Chef's obvious passion for food, and how he clearly wants us to feel it too, is pretty charming.

He takes a deep breath. "And so, we are going to split up into a few groups—get out of our ruts, yes?—and each make a different kind of pie. And to help me, I have a special guest expert today—our very own Jacqueline!"

Wait. Hold up. Chef may be charming, but our very own *who*? Jacqueline? As in, *my* mom?

Everyone looks at Mom, smiling and clapping.

Shyly, she stands up. "Hello, hello," she says, waving them off. "I am not an expert. But my granny taught me some killer Southern pies, and Chef asked me to share one with you all—or 'y'all,' as Granny would say."

OMG, my mom is doing stand-up. I try to stare her down—why didn't she tell me she was going be Chef's "special guest" today?—but I can't get her attention. Instead, she just keeps looking at Chef, shaking her head, and grinning.

Chef Antonio is practically bouncing with excitement now. "Okay, *amigos*? *Bueno.* Let us begin because we have much to do and never ever enough time. We are all going to make crust together, and it will be, as I said, *perfecto.* Then, this table over here"—he waves at one of the cooking stations—"will make a filled pie." He points to another one. "This table over here will make a two-crust apple pie, and the last table will start from scratch and make a graham-cracker crust with a key-lime filling. When we are all finished, my hope is that you will see that pie crust is nothing to be afraid of, and making it is as easy as . . . you know it . . . PIE!"

Everyone laughs, of course. Everyone except the "special guest's" daughter, a.k.a. me.

"So, *todo el mundo*—everyone—please choose your table so we may begin!"

Some people seem really sure about what kind of

pie they want to make. I stay in my seat, arms crossed, waiting to see what my mom thinks she's doing. Aren't we supposed to be taking this class together?

Errol and Henry head immediately to the one-crust pie, which is where Mom is standing. She smiles and laughs at something one of them says about Southern ladies and their pie. If I were in a better mood, I would ask her which of Granny Fran's mouthwatering pies we're talking about, but I'm not.

Tristan looks at his uncle, shrugs, and then heads over to the graham-cracker table. Following Tristan like a puppy, Frankie immediately ditches her mom, who joins mine, joking that the fewer crusts for her to ruin the better.

Dr. Wong and Lillian head to the apple-pie table with the Newlyweds. I can tell Lillian is looking around to see where Javier will go, but he's busy over at a work table cutting up butter that's been chilling in a bowl of ice for Chef Antonio. Lillian kind of trails along behind her mother, sneaking peeks at Javi every couple of seconds. If he did actually decide to choose a table right now, would she actually desert her mom and follow him? I can picture Dr. Wong's reaction to that, and it definitely wouldn't make Lillian feel less embarrassed!

I can feel Frankie's eyes boring a hole in my back, trying to get me to join her and Tristan at the graham-cracker table for moral support. I don't feel like watching her "accidentally" spill flour on his shirt or offer to show him how to properly demolish a graham cracker, so I decide to go to Mom's table after all.

"*Sí, sí, sí. Bueno.* Everybody all set?" Chef asks, taking a quick scan of the room. He spies Javier, who seems to be finished with the butter and is now just standing around wadding up towels. "No, not quite. Javi, why don't you join us?" Javier's always sort of hovering, like he can't decide whether to jump in or sneak away. He's caught now, though, so he shuffles over to the graham-cracker crew.

"The key to pie crust, *amigos*, is not to overdo it, not to overhandle it," Chef tells us. "If you do, it will be tough—leathery and chewy instead of light, feathery, and delicious! It's all about activating the gluten in the flour . . ." Chef Antonio looks around to see if we're all still paying attention. Most of the adults are, but Javier and Tristan both look pretty bored.

"*Bueno*, I'll stop now. You came here for a cooking class, not a chemistry lesson, *mi gente!*"

"You heard that, nephew?" Errol chuckles, looking over at Tristan from across the room. Embarrassed, Tristan pulls the ski cap he's been wearing all morning a little lower over his face. I am guessing he is not a fan of his chem class. Frankie stares at him as if yanking his hat down has somehow made him even cuter.

"Some people use food processors for the crust—you can try that at home," Chef continues. "Here, we are going to do it the old-fashioned way so we can get our hands dirty."

He tells us to dump the chopped-up chilled butter into our mixing bowls and add the flour. Then we pinch, pinch, pinch it until all of the little butter pellets are coated in white. Everyone is pretty focused for a while, and you can totally tell who's determined to get this right (Mom, Dr. Wong, Errol, and Margo) and who just wants to get it done (everyone else!).

Next we form balls of dough. Or some of us do—Frankie's mom, Theresa, is having trouble getting hers to come together.

"Don't worry if you still see little bits of butter," my mom explains, "you really don't want to man-handle it, T." She leans over to lend a hand, and I have to admit, in a few seconds Theresa's greasy lump actually looks like a ball of dough. Mom is really good at this.

Chef walks between all the tables, nodding happily. "Excellent. Now we chill the dough for a bit while we make the fillings. Here is where we go our separate ways for a while, *mis amigos*. Table One—I leave you with Señora Jackie. Everybody else, *vamanos!*"

Mom takes a deep breath and grins at us. "I've never taught anybody before, except of course, my children," she says, looking at me. I can tell she wants me to smile, but I'm still feeling weird about her suddenly being Chef's "special guest," and I'm not in the mood. Henry gives me a look, but I ignore him, too.

"I've been thinking a lot about my granny's favorite recipes," my mom goes on, "because Liza's got a big birthday party coming up in a few weeks, and I'm making all the desserts." *No way.* Does someone have to bring up the party *everywhere* I go? This is just getting worse and worse. Everyone at the table smiles at me, but fortunately, Mom keeps going.

"I chose this one because it's delicious, simple"— she pauses while Theresa pumps her fist—"and distinctively Southern. Buttermilk pie." She smiles. "To me, it tastes like unconditional love and comfort, so I hope you all think it's as delicious as I do!"

We gather our ingredients, which are pretty simple.

Eggs, butter, sugar, vanilla, buttermilk, flour. The next table is chopping apples for apple pie, and the graham-cracker folks are using a food processor—I guess Chef changed his mind, to keep the flying crumbs to a minimum—and melting butter. We measure and mix, using "rounded" tablespoons of flour. Mom explains that means instead of leveling off the top of the flour as we usually do, her grandmother would want us to let it heap over, or round, a little.

Theresa flings her flour all over the table as she works. "Oh, I love your grandmother, Jackie. You know, exactness really isn't my thing!"

I look over at Frankie to see if she heard her mom's understatement of the day, but she's completely focused on Tristan, as usual. "Smooth move!" she yells, punching him on the shoulder. I have no idea why, although it might have to do with the overflowing food processor that Tristan's trying to operate like it's a video game controller.

Chef brings us all our chilled balls of dough. "Let's

rock and roll, *amigos!*" he yells, handing out rolling pins to each table. Javier slumps farther down on his stool. I wonder if Chef tells those corny jokes just to make him squirm.

The two tables working with the regular dough (ours and the apple pie group) start dusting our work surfaces and rolling pins with flour. Then we start rolling. The table making graham-cracker crust presses their dough into shape in the pans instead of rolling it out. Chef gives us all pointers as he crushes some little limes in a fruit press.

"Slow and steady wins the race," Mom tells our table as we roll out our dough—it's one of her favorite expressions. Dad says that's one way you can tell she's not a native New Yorker. "Just long, even strokes with the roller. Don't whack at it, Theresa—oh my . . ."

Frankie's mom is attacking her dough more than rolling it, and it's falling apart in ugly hunks. But the rest of us are making some pretty impressive-looking slabs of dough. As she shows us how to drape them into the pans, my mom talks about cooking with her grandmother and how family occasions at Granny Fran's house meant tables piled high with homemade delicacies.

"That's why I'm excited to make the desserts for Liza's big day," she says, "because it's what the women in my family have always done. I haven't had time for much baking lately, so I really want to do it up now!" Seriously? Not this again.

To discourage my mom from saying anything else about the party, I turn my attention to the apple-pie table, where Lillian is making the most beautiful top for her pie. Chef calls it lattice, and it looks like something from a magazine. The Newlyweds are making theirs together—Margo places her pie-crust strips one way, and then Stephen layers his on top of them, so that they crisscross over each other. Margo must have bionic ears or something, though, because as soon as my mom mentions the party again, she turns and looks right at us.

"That is such a wonderful idea, Jackie," she says in her perpetually blissed-out, breathless way. I wonder if she talked like that before she and Stephen got together. "I had a big Sweet Sixteen party, and it was so lovely. There was a pink balloon tower and a disco ball." She literally sighs as she remembers it, I am not kidding. "But no one in my family is a baker, so my mom just ordered one of those big tacky cakes from the grocery store. The cake decorators even spelled my name wrong. Your plan sounds so much more personal!"

We're crimping the edges of our piecrusts now, and I'm glad to have something to focus on other than party talk. I'm using a fork like Mom told us to, but Theresa has given up and is basically just shaping her crust into the pan with her knuckles. Mom tries to show her how to rub a little water into the dough to fix all the holes and tears, but Theresa just grabs little pieces of dough and smooshes them over the problems.

"I loved my Sweet Sixteen." Theresa sighs as she attempts to sloppily patch another hole. "I danced with Joe all night. I'm sure Mama and Nonna cooked up a storm for the party, but I don't even remember the food. At the time it was the most romantic night of my life . . ." She actually starts humming that song from The *Sound of Music* about being sixteen going on seventeen.

Okay, hold up. I'm turning thirteen, not sixteen, and I'm definitely not looking for a magical night of romance. Unlike my two best friends, I don't even have a crush! Suddenly everyone is reminiscing about their favorite birthday bashes—Errol's sister had one, Henry's cousin, even Dr. Wong has some stories about parties back in San Francisco. Lillian and Frankie shoot me sympathetic looks, but they're as powerless as I am against the birthday brigade. . . .

At last there's a distraction as Angelica carries Cole over to one of the giant refrigerators to get him some juice. While she's pouring, he runs to our table and begs Mom for some dough (when she does bake, she always gives him some pieces to play with). My brother's like a frisky puppy, and everyone seems to want to give him little scraps. Some he balls up in his hand, but he eats quite a bit of it too. I don't blame him—raw dough is delicious, even though you're not supposed to eat uncooked eggs and all that. Angelica stops to admire Lillian's handiwork and then catches on to what everyone is talking about.

"A party? *Que bueno!* I just had the one son, but I always wanted to plan a *quinceañera*. . . . In Cuba we celebrate the girl's fifteenth birthday, not the sixteenth, you know. It's a night to remember, and I wished always to give one." She scoops up Cole and spins him around like he's Prince Charming, which makes him bubble with laughter as always. Chef steps around them as he circles the tables and pretends to look hurt.

"Sorry, Mami, that I was not a little girl for you.

Maybe we can dress up Javi for his *quinceañera* and pretend? Ha!"

Okay, well at least now there's officially someone in the room more horrified than I am. But why is Javier over there chuckling with Tristan instead of burying himself in his hoodie? Boy bonding? Where are my BFFs when I need them?

I spin around to find Lillian alternately obsessing over her perfect lattice and sneaking looks at Javier. At the graham-cracker table, Frankie's pouring key-lime filling into the crust while Tristan holds the pan. She's trying to gaze into his eyes, but he is more interested in scanning the table for crumbs and tossing them into his mouth. Meanwhile, Frankie's not even using a spoon to scrape up the leftover filling, which is totally unlike her. Something is definitely up with Frankie.

Mom puts the last of our buttermilk pies into the big ovens, and when she turns around I see that she has a flour smudge on the tip of her nose. Before I can tell her, Chef Antonio swoops over and dusts it off with his oven mitt. They both laugh, but I'm not amused. First, the party I'm not in the least bit excited about takes over our Saturday cooking club, and now my mom and Chef are acting weird. The only good thing about this stupid not-mitzvah is that my parents are starting to like each other again. Our handsome, charming TV star Chef had better not get in the way. . . .

CHAPTER 11
Frankie

My dad sent me to the vegetable stand on Court Street to get a whole bunch of different-colored peppers and some onions. Of course, thanks to Chef Antonio and the cooking class, I now know that peppers are actually fruit, not veggies, but I'm not about to tell Mr. Pak that he should change the name of his stand. I love that Dad trusts me to pick out the best ones— he's super choosy about his ingredients and usually spends way too much time studying, squeezing, and sniffing the merchandise at Mr. Pak's. But today is Sunday and he's trying to crank out a mess of dinners for the week, since he'll be on duty at the firehouse until eight or nine almost every night. I like to go to the vegetable stand and do my best Joe Caputo impression, inspecting the vegetables for perfection. I like to think I can spot perfection pretty easily—it's one of my talents.

My dad dedicating an entire day to cooking for the week spares us the ordeal of Mom making dinner. True fact: She's not as bad as she used to be. But when you're talking about my mom, that doesn't mean much. The cooking class has helped a bit, I have to admit. Most things she tries these days are pretty much cooked all the way through—a big improvement—and she *might* not hurt herself every single time. Still, she's not the greatest at following a recipe, she hasn't exactly perfected her technique when it comes to slicing and dicing, and she's not what you'd call "relaxed" in the kitchen—she bangs pots and pans and swears (under her breath), which makes it all the more difficult to enjoy the . . . somewhat edible . . . results. Soooo, we all do whatever we can to help Dad stockpile.

When my dad cooks, the house smells amazing, and he just totally gets into this zone. It sounds weird, but it's actually a great time to talk to him because he's so focused on what he's doing, it's like his mind is free to think about other things. So, on his marathon cooking days, I usually end up hanging out in the kitchen, playing sous-chef to Dad, and chatting about stuff. Today, however, I'm not feeling the urge to help him layer pasta or sauté onions and garlic or roast chickens. None of it sounds very appealing. Even picking and choosing the vegetables (or fruit, to be exact) like a judge on *The Voice* didn't cheer me up. On my way home I trudge past all the same sturdy brownstones I've seen all my life, toward the spikes of the black iron fence in front of our house, and all of the bikes, scooters, and skateboards locked to its spindles. Stepping over huge muddy puddles left over from yesterday's rain, I already know exactly what will happen when I open the door. The Goons will be crashing through the house, shaking the walls and floors with their stomping and bellowing (no matter how much Mom begs them to "use your inside voices"). Nicky will be playing Ancient Heroes without paying attention to where he's going and will knock something over with a sword or a shield or, more likely, both. Our house, as usual, will be entirely *feng shui* free.

Still feeling weird, I take Dad his ingredients. He's blasting some radio station that's playing All Eighties Music All the Time and tries to get me to dance with him. Um, no. Not today. Nicky bursts in and says he needs aluminum foil to make silver wings for his shoes like the Greek god Hermes, so while Dad digs around for the foil, I decide to take cover in my room.

I race up the stairs but, of course, The Goons are

blocking my way at the top, arguing over who gets control of the remote. As usual, some big game is happening somewhere, and one of them absolutely *has* to watch it, while the other one wants to play video games.

"Move it," I say, trying to get around them as they shove each other. "Move your stupid fight off the stairs now. You goons are going to hurt somebody."

"Yeah, right." Leo chuckles to Joey without even looking at me. "Like falling down the stairs would even hurt you, Chubbers. You'd just bounce."

Okay, fine, so I was a chunky baby and my "affectionate" family nickname was Chubbers. So what. That was a long time ago in a body far far away. I push through them, hoping maybe I'll knock one of them down a step or two. But no, they don't seem to notice. They storm off downstairs, continuing their stupid battle over the Golden Remote the entire time. I have no idea how my relatively normal mom (outside of the kitchen) and my nice-guy dad managed to produce such total idiots.

Mom calls to me. She's in my parents' bedroom folding laundry (pretty much a full-time job around here) and she smiles at me as I come in. "Hey, there. Aren't you usually chopping and stirring and packing up a freezer full of dinners downstairs with Dad?"

I shrug as she continues matching up socks with a practiced eye. Who can tell the difference between all those Goon-size gym socks? Or those black, brown, and blue ones my dad always wears? My mom can.

"Why so glum, bella?" she asks, using the nickname I usually love. I shrug again and she comes over to squeeze my shoulder.

"Okay, okay. Are your brothers bothering you? You know they just live to tease, don't pay them any attention." I shake my head. For some reason I'm having trouble speaking up.

"Maybe just some Sunday blahs? Sundays can be so depressing, right? With everyone trying desperately to cram in the last precious seconds of the weekend before finishing homework and getting things organized for the week." I don't bother reminding her that with the exception of laundry and dinners, few things are ever "organized" in this house—on Sunday or any other day.

My mom keeps trying. "I know what will cheer you up. Tell me what to wear to my parent-teacher conferences next week. Help me dazzle the parents of my second graders in the way that only you can. I need all the help I can get . . . " She keeps talking, but I've stopped listening. Usually this is the kind of thing I live for, telling people what to wear, coming up with the best possible combinations, putting outfits together.

I stand in front of my parents' closet, crowded with their clothes, a bunch of Dad's big bulky firemen uniforms hanging there like deflated men, and all sorts of old school projects of ours (an ancient papier-mâché Empire State building made by one

Goon, an electrical circuit made by the other, my Terracotta Warrior from the China unit in third grade, and Nicky's marble maze are all crammed into corners and onto shelves), and I realize this closet is like a time capsule version of my crazy family and our sprawling mess of a house. Now there's no way I can focus. It doesn't matter what skirt and cardigan combo I pick out for my mom—she'll still be the same old easy-going Theresa, working mother of four, who chooses not to notice the chaos that surrounds her. She'll never understand everything that's wrong in my world. She just doesn't get why for once I just want things to be calm and perfect. Perfectly calm.

"I can't help," I manage to say as I shake my head and race out the door.

"Francesca . . ." I hear as I run down the narrow hall. Not today, Mom, not today.

When I get to my room, I pull out my phone to call Liza. It's a reflex, really—something happens to me and *bam*, I call her. But then I realize, nothing has happened. Nothing just happened that hasn't happened a million times before. My dad is cooking. My brothers are fighting. My mom is minding her own business, folding laundry.

I throw myself onto the bed with its faded strawberry-pattern sheet set that I've had since I was eight and pull my pillows over my head. *Something has got to change.* And if my life isn't going to change on its own, I need to *make* it change. I need to be the Frankie that has something new to say, someplace interesting to be, something important to be doing.

Whoa. I sit straight up, dropping my strawberry-speckled pillow to the floor. The answer is so obvious: I need to be more like Lillian's sister, Katie. Perfect Katie, who knows exactly who she is and where she's going. There are flyers in the halls at school for track-team tryouts. I can learn how to run, and breathe, and be focused, just like her. It just takes willpower and practice.

And practice makes perfect!

CHAPTER 12
Liza

After a few amazingly springlike days, Mother Nature apparently remembered it's still February (a.k.a. cold and damp), so we haven't had lunch in the quad for ages. On Wednesdays I have PE right before lunch, which means I'm still changing out of my gym uniform when the bell rings. By the time I get to the cafeteria, Frankie and Lillian are already camped out at our usual table. Even from halfway across the room I can tell by the looks on their faces that they're talking about

Tristan and Javier. I'm glad the two of them are bonding over their cooking class crushes, but I hope we're not going to spend the entire lunch period debating the relative cuteness of Tristan's eyes or Javier's smile.

"Liza!" Frankie chirps as I plop my gym bag down on one chair and my still-slightly-sweaty self on another. "Wasn't it super cute when Tristan gave Cole a high five on Saturday?"

"Mmm," I say with a nod, digging into my rice and beans (forty-five minutes of dodgeball and I am *starving*), "adorbs."

Lillian grabs my wrist. "And don't you think Javier makes the funniest expressions when Chef embarrasses him in class?"

"Yeah," I say, hoping she'll let go so I can take another bite. "He's pretty hilarious."

I guess my answers weren't enthusiastic enough, because Frankie and Lillian go back to chatting with each other about the boys. I don't mean to be unsupportive, but I have other things on my mind right now, like how to stop Nana from turning my birthday party into the social event of the year for the over-sixty crowd, and how to keep my mom and dad in this happy place so that maybe they'll actually get back together again.

My container of rice and beans is already practically empty, but for some reason I'm still hungry. Lillian's slurping up the last few noodles from her thermos, but there's a delicious-looking stuffed shell in front of Frankie that she's barely even touched. When she's not going on about how great Tristan is, she's nibbling on baby carrots and slices of cucumber—two things I'm pretty sure I've never seen in her lunch bag before.

"If you don't stop talking and start eating, I'm going to steal that," I say, pointing to the stuffed shell.

Frankie waves me off. "Go for it," she says, sliding the container across the table. "I'm not really hungry. And this stuff is all there is to eat at my house. It's like they've never heard of a balanced diet."

"Seriously, Franks? You're not going to start obsessing about dieting, are you?"

Frankie looks down at her carrots. "I'm just eating like I care about my body for a change, instead of just mindlessly shoveling it in like some people I live with. There's nothing wrong with that."

"There is if you start sounding like my sister. And if it means you're missing out on your dad's amazing stuffed shell," Lillian says, shrugging. "But more for us I guess." She messily stabs a hunk with her chopstick and almost drops it right smack in the middle of her flawless cream-colored sweater.

"A little dose of your sister would work wonders at my house. But whatever—can we have a conversation about something else?" Frankie snaps, shoving her bag of veggies into her backpack.

"Um, yeah," I say. "Totally. You guys have been blabbing away about the boys from cooking class for the past ten minutes."

Frankie and Lillian look at each other and then back at me.

"Sorry, Liza," Lillian says. "You must be sick of

hearing about Tristan and Javier by now. I think even I'm a little sick of it."

"A little," I shrug.

"Me too. Forget them," says Frankie. "*Soooo*, let's talk about what's going on in your life, Lize. How's party planning? Has Nana Silver decided on normal boring paper invitations, or a giant billboard with your face lit up ten stories high in the middle of Times Square?"

Lillian laughs, but I practically have a heart attack.

"Promise me you won't ever make that joke around Nana, Frankie. You'll give her ideas."

Frankie rolls her eyes. "Oh, come on, Liza. She's not *that* bad."

"I didn't think she would be," I say, "but now I'm not so sure. She's talking about hiring a personal shopper to put together the goodie bags."

"Oooh, I love goodie bags," Lillian says, clapping excitedly. "I mean, I love the idea of them. I've never actually gotten a *real* goodie bag—just the ones filled with junky plastic toys from little-kid birthday parties."

Frankie leans forward, practically putting her elbow in her lunch.

"Liza and I got *amazing* goodie bags at this party for the tenth anniversary of her mom's magazine. There were all kinds of makeup samples and hair stuff—there was even some sexy lacy underwear in every bag because one of the sponsors of the party was Victoria Secret or something. But her mom wouldn't let us keep those, because we were only nine."

"I would have been so embarrassed!" Lillian says, covering her mouth with her hand as if she could get in trouble for just thinking about it. Of course, with a mother as strict as hers, maybe she could.

"Not me," says Frankie. "I wanted to keep them!"

"Well, there will *not* be underwear of any kind in the goodie bags at my birthday party," I say firmly. "But it's a total mystery to me what Nana's personal shopper is going to come up with. The one thing I do know is that there's basically a zero-percent chance anyone will ask for my opinion."

"I hope there's makeup," says Lillian, less interested in my party angst than the possibility of high-quality loot. "Not that my mom will ever let me wear it."

"She'll let you wear a little to the party, won't she?" Frankie asks. "Just lipstick, or some mascara? Just a tiny bit? Your eyes would really pop."

"No way, she's super strict about her No-Makeup-Until-You're-Sixteen rule. But since it is such a fancy event, I really want to dress up, so maybe . . ."

And once again, my two best friends are talking about my party like it's a *good* thing. Why don't they understand that it's destined to be a disaster of epic proportions?

I slide the container with the remains of the shell in front of me and dig in. If ever I needed comfort food, it's now.

CHAPTER 13
Liza

Health class is just ending when I feel my phone vibrate in my pocket. I'm hoping it's Frankie or Lillian so I can tell them how Mr. Lewis—whose breath smells like moldy cheese—gave his famous lecture on halitosis today. The guy teaches a unit on the importance of oral hygiene every year, and he still has the foulest breath in the school!

Unfortunately, when I get out in the hallway and check my phone, the text isn't from Frankie or

Lillian—it's from Nana Silver. Nana must have just discovered texting, because until now she's only called me, and even that she still does from landline to landline. Clearly she's in need of Texting Etiquette 101, because her message is all in caps and during the school day—though knowing Nana, she probably thinks whatever she has to say is incredibly urgent and important.

LIZA NANA HERE.

As if I didn't know.

FOUND AN EXCELLENT LETTERPRESS STUDIO. FOR INVITATIONS. HAVE AN APPOINTMENT AT 4 PM. TAXI WILL BE WAITING IN FRONT OF SCHOOL AT 3:15 SHARP. DON'T BE LATE. LOVE

I've never read an actual old-fashioned telegram, but for some reason Nana's text reminds me of one. I can almost see her dictating it to some guy in a bowtie and cap. "Liza Nana Here STOP Don't be late STOP."

Frankie and I are supposed to go over to Lillian's

house this afternoon to do homework, but I can't exactly say no to Nana Silver. I mean, I could, of course, but I'd rather just go along with her last-minute "invitation" than try to survive her guilt-laying superpowers. I text Frankie and Lillian (the normal way—with the caps lock *off*) and tell them not to bother picking me up at my locker because I'm being whisked away to a thrilling afternoon of stationery shopping.

When the final bell rings, I shove everything I need for homework into my backpack and make a beeline for the exit. As soon as I push through the doors, I see the taxi waiting right out front, just like Nana said it would be. Most kids walk or take the subway to school, so I feel really weird getting picked up by a waiting taxi. I hope no one thinks this is how I normally get around.

I get in and give Nana a quick hug. She smells like she always does, Chanel No. 5—she's probably been wearing it since it was invented. "It's my signature scent," Nana told me once, when I asked her if she ever thought about trying something new—as if Coco Chanel had created it just for her.

Nana squeezes my hand. "You're going to love these invitations, Liza. I think they're just perfect and I can't wait for you to see them."

Can't think of anything I'd rather be doing, I think to myself, holding in a sigh and trying to smile.

In case you're wondering, a letterpress is a machine that presses words and designs into paper so that they stick out a little on the front in 3-D, and when you run your hand over the paper, you can actually feel the letters. I only know this because Joan, the woman who owns the letterpress studio Nana thinks is "divine," has just explained the entire process to me, step-by-step. To be honest, it's actually pretty cool, and it's obvious that Joan and her husband Randy live for this stuff. But I can tell by the look on Nana Silver's face that I'm not showing quite enough enthusiasm about it.

"So what do you think, darling," Nana asks, holding up a pair of identical sample invitations written in very frilly script that I can hardly read, "silver or gold? I prefer the gold, but the silver is more casual, which I know is more your style."

I'm not sure I even have a "style," but if I do, this invitation is definitely not it, regardless of which metallic shade it's printed in.

"Does it have to be in cursive, Nana? Kids my age hardly ever write that way, you know."

Nana crosses her arms and looks at me like I've just delivered the news that her cat has two months to live. "Well, that's a travesty," she says. "Add that to the list of the failures of public education. And all the more reason you should choose an invitation that exposes your classmates to proper penmanship."

"I think you'll both find this font to be very attractive," Joan says, showing us another sample.

I learned about fonts when I started doing assignments for school on the computer, but I didn't know people actually talked about them in the real world. I guess if your job is to figure out how to make words look pretty, you have to get more creative than just Times New Roman and Arial.

Surprisingly, Joan is right. The letters on this sample are in a roundish, friendly-looking print that's sort of like a professional version of Lillian's perfect handwriting—a little girly, but not overly cutesy.

Nana, however, is clearly unimpressed. "For a casual summer picnic or a potluck dinner, maybe," she says, wrinkling her nose. "But to announce the celebration of a young girl beginning her journey into womanhood? I don't think so."

I practically gag when Nana mentions my "journey into womanhood." What does that even mean, anyway? I'm only in seventh grade. I'm not even an official teenager yet, much less a woman!

While Nana is flipping through samples, I raise my eyebrows at Joan to let her know I'm aware that my grandmother isn't the easiest customer. She smiles and rolls her eyes as if to say, "Don't worry, I deal with this all the time," and I decide I like her more than I expected to.

"You know," Joan says, digging deep into a drawer I haven't seen her open before, "you might like this one." She takes a large square envelope out of the drawer and pulls a thick pale-gray invitation from it. "I designed it for our wedding."

Joan and Randy smile at each other as I take the invitation from her hand. They may be super serious about stationary, but they're still a pretty cute couple.

The handwriting—I mean font—is miraculously somewhere between print and script, and I actually really like it. Clearly, Joan gets "the look" a girl my age would go for. I wish I could say the same for Nana Silver.

"Hmm, well," she says, taking off her reading glasses and holding the invitation out about a foot from her face—as if that's how anyone reads. "I'm sure your wedding guests found this just lovely, but the lines are so thin, someone of my . . . maturity . . . would need a magnifying glass just to read it."

I make eye contact with Joan again, who smiles just a little to let me know it's okay, she's used to it. Nana catches us and sighs dramatically. Uh-oh.

"Of course, if that's really what Liza wants, well then, who I am to deprive her?" she says. "Who am I to suggest that my friends' fading vision should trump my granddaughter's aesthetic preferences?"

And Nana for the win. I take a deep breath.

"You know what, Nana? Let's just go with the one you like—the cursive. It's pretty. And anyway, it's just the invitation, right?"

I notice Randy wrinkle his brow just a bit.

"I mean, no offense," I say quickly, looking from Randy to Joan to let them know I wasn't dissing their entire life's work. "The invitations are import-ant, of course, it's just that we have so many things to decide on for the party, I'm okay with Nana pick-ing out this one."

Nana Silver smiles at me and then reaches for her wallet. "Such a dear, isn't she?" she says to Joan as she hands her a credit card. Happy as a clam at last, Nana cups my chin in her hand. "And so gorgeous, too, don't you think?"

My cheeks burn beneath Nana's long, smooth fingers, but Joan catches my eye and smiles one last time. "Beautiful," she says, handing my grandmother the receipt to sign and giving me a little wink. "She looks just like you."

CHAPTER 14
Liza

I'm slicing up a banana for Cole when my mom comes into the kitchen to get some coffee. It's eleven thirty and we're still in our pajamas. Mom's been at the computer doing some work she brought home with her, while Cole and I have been watching our favorite *Sesame Street* episodes back to back. I say "our favorite" because it's true—I'm almost thirteen years old and I'm not ashamed to admit that I still like *Sesame Street*. I mean, I doubt I'd watch it if I didn't have a little brother, but I'm glad I have that as an excuse. I'm pretty sure I'm not the only *Sesame Street* fan who's over five—tons of really big celebrities have done guest spots, and you can tell they're having loads of fun performing with the Muppets.

"I'm glad you two have something in common still . . . ," my mom says as she adds some milk from the cup I just poured for Cole into her mug, "but I think that's more than enough TV for one morning."

I'm about to point out that she's been working for two straight hours without Cole yelling "Mommy!" once, when her phone rings and our *Sesame Street* marathon is temporarily saved by the bell.

After she says, "Hello, this is Jacqueline," all businesslike, my mom's voice softens and I can tell whoever's on the other end is a friend. It doesn't take long for me to figure out who it is: after about three seconds Mom says, "Oh, that sounds like Nana, all right," and I know she's talking to my dad.

I decide to make myself some toast so I have an

excuse to hang around the kitchen while they're on the phone. It doesn't matter that I can only hear half of the conversation—the fact that my parents are actually laughing and joking with each other instead of talking about tense things like daycare bills and dividing school vacations is enough to tell me that I wasn't imagining things the last time I heard them talk about the party. My mom and dad *really are* getting along— and if putting up with a few more weeks of letterpress studios and party venues is what it takes to keep them that way, then Nana Silver can bring it on.

We have a really nice walk to cooking class—no torrential downpours this week—and Mom's been in an upbeat mood all morning, despite the fact that she had to do work on a Saturday, which she hates. She's smiling and actually humming as we walk, so she must still be thinking about my dad's call. My mom is usually all about jeans and worn-in comfy tops on the weekends, but today she's wearing one of her casual-Friday skirts and tops. She says it was the rare sunny Saturday that put her in the mood, but I'd bet my brother's fancy new "big-kid" stroller that talking to my dad is what did it.

We run into Henry, Errol, and Tristan on the way to the studio. In class, Tristan is usually pretty quiet and, other than barely responding to Frankie, he doesn't say much to anyone, including his uncle. But walking down the block all three of them look and sound like old pals, laughing about some fly-fishing adventure they apparently went on together. (I don't know much about fly fishing, but from what I can tell it involves a lot of standing around in a river waiting for the fish to come to you—not exactly my thing.) I guess around just Henry and Errol, Tristan has a lot more personality than I thought. In cooking class, he must think it's uncool to act buddy-buddy with your uncle. Or maybe he's just shy? It's hard to imagine someone that good-looking has anything to be shy about. He and Javier may have more in common than I thought.

"*Ah, mis amigas favoritas,*" Chef Antonio greets my mom and me as we file into the studio. His favorite friends, huh?

"And Ms. Jacqueline is looking especially lovely today," he continues, taking her coat.

Mom smiles shyly as I think to myself, *That's right, you noticed. And it's all thanks to Dad.*

Cole is excited to show off his new stroller, so Angelica skips unbuckling him and wheels him away to their corner like it's a race car.

My mom and I take seats at a long table with Frankie, Theresa, Lillian, and Dr. Wong. It feels just like old times, except both Frankie and Lillian keep stealing glances at their crushes. I hope they'll give it a rest while we're actually cooking.

"*Bienvenidos* my friends, to our first savory class of the session," Chef announces to get our attention. "Last week we made dessert pies, but this week we'll be making pastries that are intended as main courses, side dishes, or *bocadillos rápidos*—quick and tasty snacks."

I look at Lillian and Frankie—snacks are our thing. Lillian rubs her hands together eagerly, but Frankie just sort of half smiles. What is her deal lately?

Since we all "perfected" our crust making last week (though I'm not sure Theresa's would fit that description), Chef shows us a giant bowl of balls of dough that he and Javier mixed up for us to use today.

"It was a true bonding experience for *papi* and *hijo*," he says, resting his hand on Javier's shoulder. "Don't you agree, *mijo*?" Javier gives a quick nod and then looks over at Tristan and rolls his eyes. Tristan rolls his in sympathy. Boys.

Chef Antonio steps away from the table and holds out the bowl of dough. "And the results, *mis amigos*, mean that we can spend our time filling, baking, and eating today, rather than kneading and rolling. *Bueno*?"

Frankie's mom sighs so loudly that everyone turns to look at her. "*Sí, muy bien!*" she says. "Thank God."

We all laugh, even Tristan and Javier. Even Frankie—despite the fact that she's probably totally embarrassed. Or maybe she's just used to her mother's humor by now.

Chef strolls to our table and puts his arm around Theresa. "I'm glad you are relieved, *señora!*" he says. "Nothing gives me more pleasure than to put people at ease *en la cocina*—the kitchen."

"Anyway," Chef continues, letting go of Theresa and moving to the head of our table, next to my mom. "Our first project of the day will be pot pies."

There's a general rumble of approval throughout the room. Who doesn't love a pot pie? Even our school cafeteria—which is famous for its limp, lukewarm, utterly flavorless meals—serves up a halfway decent chicken pot pie. On a cold gray day in February, like the ones we've been having the past few weeks, I've actually looked forward to the moment a shockingly hot and flaky CPP is plunked onto my tray.

"It just so happens that we have some very tender

and juicy *pollo asado*—roast chicken—leftover from yesterday's taping. Trust me, it may have spent the night in the fridge, but it's delicious."

Suddenly Margo springs from her chair. "We saw that episode!" she cries, giving Stephen's shoulder a tug. "It made us so hungry we actually went shopping and cooked a second dinner."

"I saw it, too," says Henry. "Looked divine."

"I agree," says a voice from our table. We all look to see who it was, and I'm pretty sure we're equally stunned to discover it is Lillian's mother. Dr. Wong watches *Antonio's Kitchen*? When we first started taking the class back in the fall, she could hardly walk into class without giving him a lecture of her own. And now she's a fan of his TV show? I suppose weirder things have happened, but I'm having a hard time thinking of any.

Beaming, Chef steps behind Lillian's mom and puts his hands on her shoulders. She looks a little uncomfortable with the physical contact, but manages a half smile anyway. *"Oh, mis amigos,"* Chef says, giving Dr. Wong's shoulders a light squeeze, "you were all watching the show? I'm so touched."

"We never miss it," Margo calls out as Dr. Wong gives Chef's hand a stiff, awkward pat.

Still smiling like he's just won an Oscar, Chef Antonio moves back to the head of our table. "I'm flattered, *mis estudiantes,* I cannot lie. So yes, anyway, the chicken is very tasty. Let us mix it with the fresh vegetables you see on your tables"—he gestures to the large bowls piled high with carrots, onions, and potatoes—"and believe it or not, even some frozen ones." He picks up smaller bowls filled with bright green peas and yellow corn. "If it was summer, we would be using fresh, of course, but trust me, our pot pies will be *delicioso* just the same."

Chef Antonio pauses to reach for a small round baking dish—I'm pretty sure its smooth white surface is called porcelain—from one of the prep tables behind him. Then he puts one hand on my mom's shoulder and hands her the dish with the other.

"And now, since she was such a *fantástica* assistant last week, I'll ask our *amiga* Jackie to *ayúdame*—help me—once again by demonstrating how to make the lovely circles of dough that will serve as protective—and delightful—little blankets over our savory ingredients."

My mom raises her eyebrows and gives Chef a look that says, "Who me?" but she doesn't waste any time getting up. "Well," she says to the room, as if she does this kind of thing every day, "it's been a while, but from the time I was even younger than Liza, I can remember a lot of Saturday afternoons spent at Momma's table cutting out piecrusts." Then she rolls one of the balls of dough from the giant bowl into a thin slab and uses the upside-down baking dish as a giant cookie cutter to make a perfect circle for the top of a pot pie. Not one tear. Impeccable. I catch Theresa shaking her head in disbelief.

Everyone claps, as if my mom is a surgeon who's

just successfully sewn back on a patient's ear, rather than a woman who comes from a long line of bakers and has a talent for cutting out piecrusts. "Aww, stop it," she says, letting the southern drawl she famously spent all four years of college trying to conquer slip out just a bit. "Y'all are making me blush."

And here we go again. It may still be a sunny Saturday outside, but now that today's class is shaping up to be a replay of last week's *Antonio & Jackie Show*, it's feeling more like a soggy gray Sunday inside every minute.

My mom floats around the tables helping some people cut out crusts while the rest of us stir up our veggies in big pots on the stove with some broth, butter, and flour. When the carrots and potatoes have just started to get tender, we add some of the shredded leftover chicken (which is exactly as delicious as everyone says—I couldn't help myself, I had to try it). When the filling is ready, we pour it into little dishes chef calls "crock pots" (weird name or what?) and then drape the delicate piecrust circles over the filling. Frankie won't let Theresa anywhere near the dough, while at the other side of the table Dr. Wong is literally hovering over Lillian as she very carefully places her crusts over the pots and pinches the sides to seal in the filling.

Mom pops back to our table to show us how to make little slits in the dough to let out the steam while the pot pies bake. Chef calls everyone else over to watch.

"Now those, *mi gente*, are perfect incisions," he proclaims, his smile so big it's gleaming.

"Oh, go on, now stop," my mom says, but it's clear she's enjoying herself. "Everyone can do that."

"Not everyone," Frankie mutters under her breath. Theresa shoots her a look.

"You two should take your show on the road," Errol says to my mom and Chef Antonio.

"Or on TV!" Margo chimes in. "You make such a great team."

"Hmm, *buena idea*," Chef strokes his chin. "I'll have to talk to my producers." He's teasing (I hope), but I can tell my mom is flattered.

"Please," Mom says, "I already have one job and two kids—another job and the bags under my eyes will be carrying bags." She gives Chef a little shove, and he pretends to practically fall over.

Maybe Nana should hire them to perform their little routine at my party.

CHAPTER 15
Lillian

I think Chef Antonio sensed a little mother-daughter tension at our table—I know I did—so after the pot pies he decided we needed to "stir things up" as he likes to say. He actually made everyone put their names in a hat (a chef's hat, of course!) and then he asked Liza's mom, his "assistant," to pick out four names at a time and put them at each of the tables. Don't ask me how, but for some reason Frankie wound up at a table with Tristan, and I ended up with Javier!

Liza and Henry are also at my table, and Liza's mom and Margo are at Frankie's. I can tell Mama's not all that comfortable in her group, which includes Errol, Mrs. Caputo—I mean Theresa—and Stephen. Even though she's sitting at a different table than I am, she keeps pushing her chair closer to mine and watching everything I'm doing. As if being paired up with Javier weren't stressful enough!

While my mom keeps an eye on me, I'm doing my best to sneak peeks at Frankie and Tristan without being too obvious about it. I'm hoping to get some ideas for how to talk to or act around Javier, since my usual approach of saying practically nothing isn't exactly a recipe for romance. Mostly, I notice Frankie pretending to "accidentally" swipe Tristan's hat, or knock him off his chair. It's totally impressive the way she's not shy at all, but I can't really tell if he thinks it's funny, or cute, or maybe a little . . . annoying. Still, at least they're actually talking to each other, unlike Javier and me. . . .

Chef Antonio bangs a wooden spoon on a big stainless-steel bowl to get our attention. "Now that we're in our new groups and out of our comfort zone a bit," he begins (and he is so right!), "we will find our inspiration for our next recipe in the beautiful country of France."

Frankie looks over at Liza. Ever since they were little they've had this "grand plan" to go to Paris together when they're eighteen. Now that all three of us are friends, if they ever do actually end up going, I hope they take me with them.

"The *galette* is a free-form pastry that originated in the French countryside, and it is both *exquisito* to eat and very simple to make." Chef says this last part directly to Theresa, who smiles. I see her look over at Frankie, but she's too busy trying to knock Tristan off his propped up elbow to notice. Like we did for the pot pies, we're using dough that Chef and Javier already made. I'm a little disappointed that we're not starting the dough from scratch again like last week.

I actually really liked the whole process of starting with the butter, adding the flour, pinching it together, and rolling it out—it was what Tanya, our gym teacher, would call "meditative," I think. She's training to become a certified yoga instructor, and she's always talking about the benefits of meditation. I don't think I ever really understood what she meant until last week when we were working with the dough.

According to Chef Antonio, with galettes you apparently don't need to worry about how even the dough is, or how perfectly you slice it. That's great news for Theresa, for sure, but not so much for my mother, who is big on order and doesn't really get the concept of "free-form." Javier, on the other hand, seems totally into it.

"I've made these with my dad before," he says to me (to me!). "They're really cool—you can stuff them with anything."

"Anything?" Liza asks. "You mean like, even Cheerios?" She's kidding, I think. Sometimes it's

THE SATURDAY COOKING CLUB

still hard for me to tell when Liza and Frankie are being sarcastic. My best friend, Sierra, back home in San Francisco, says it's an East Coast–West Coast thing. Back in California people don't use sarcasm as much as they do here. It's taken me a while to get used to it.

"Sure," Javier says. "If you like your pies dry and crunchy. I like mine with tomatoes, sausage, and cheese—kind of like a French pizza."

I clear my throat and force myself to actually look at Javier when I speak. "How about pickles?" I ask, hoping it sounds funny and not totally stupid.

Javier actually laughs! "Well, I guess they could work. If you like your pickles hot and covered in pie crust."

I wrinkle my nose. "Not really," I say. "I think your pizza idea is better."

Javier and Liza nod their heads in agreement.

"Well, folks," Henry says, pointing to a bowl of something purple in the middle of our table, "if I'm not mistaken, I believe we're going to be filling our galettes with beets this afternoon."

"*Exactamente!*" cries Chef, who has been standing behind our table the entire time. He turns to the rest of the class. "Because the beet is a bit messy to prepare—purple stains on aprons are okay, but on my brand-new appliances? No, no, no—I've done the work of roasting and peeling them for you." He holds up his hands and shows off his still-purple fingers. "And trust me, it was not such a pretty sight."

I look over at Frankie and see her dip her finger into the bowl of beets and then poke the back of Tristan's hand, leaving a purple smudge. Tristan makes a face, but then does the same thing back to Frankie. They make spots on each other's clean white aprons until Ms. Reynolds, who's also at their table, pulls the beets out of their reach and gives them a look. The whole thing reminds me of the time Sierra and I got in trouble with our kindergarten teacher for being too messy with our finger paint. Still, we were five years old and Frankie and Tristan are, well, not.

Chef tells us to chop up Brussels sprouts and sauté them with some onion until they're soft. Then we roll out a sheet of dough and drop what he calls a "dollop" of goat cheese on top of it. Javier, Liza, and I joke around about how big a dollop actually is—is it the size of an ice-cream scoop? a spoonful of peanut butter? a squirt of shaving cream?—until Chef actually comes to our table and demonstrates (a scoop of ice cream was our closest guess). Liza pours our Brussels sprouts on top of the cheese, and then Henry adds some beets. (I think the adults have made a secret pact to keep the beets away from the kids after Frankie and Tristan's smudge-fight.) Once all of the ingredients are in, I fold the dough around the sides to form the galette.

Javier says, "Nice job," and actually pats me on the back (!) before pinching the folded edges here and there. He doesn't often remind me of Chef, but when he makes his little "improvements," he looks and acts just like him. Liza watches and smiles at me—she must be thinking the same thing.

While the galettes bake, Chef Antonio gives each table the option of making savory bread pudding or cheese straws. At our table Henry is the only one who votes for bread pudding—there's something about the name, even, that's not exactly appetizing—but he's a good sport about being outvoted by the kids.

Javier assures us that we made the right choice, because his dad's cheese straws are "mad good." Liza and I roll our eyes when he says it—sometimes he tries to act or talk like he's tougher than he is, and it comes out sounding more silly than cool. I know it's kind of lame that he does it, but I can't help thinking it's cute, too.

To make the cheese straws, we start by grating extra-sharp cheddar cheese (my favorite kind— although all cheeses are pretty much my favorites), and then we add some flour and chilled butter. On top of that we toss in salt, cayenne pepper, and a little bit of milk.

"This is a recipe for those of us who like to get our hands dirty," Chef says, looking at Frankie and Tristan, who are also making cheese straws.

Henry leaves it to the three of us to dig our hands into the batter and mix it until the ingredients feel like "coarse meal." I'm not sure Liza, Javier, or I have ever felt coarse meal before, exactly, but when we think we're pretty close, we add some more milk, and then we make a big ball out of the dough. We toss some flour on our pastry board, and Henry rolls out the dough. Then we each take turns making long, thin strips with a pizza cutter.

"Twist them if you dare to try, *mis amigos*," Chef says. That sounds like a challenge, so of course we do.

It's not until we're twisting our last few straws that I realize I haven't seen or heard from my mother since we started making the galettes. Spinning around in my seat to see what she's up to, I am shocked to see her at the head of her table, stirring up a big bowl of bread pudding and shouting out assignments to her group mates. I mean, it's totally like Mama to take charge in the kitchen, but usually it's her own kitchen and she's ordering around her own children, not other adults. Of course, Theresa is happy to follow my mother's instructions—and bread pudding seems like the safer choice for her than twisty cheese straws—but it's funny to see Stephen and Errol following Mama's lead as well. She must be enjoying herself, since she won't be teaching college kids again until next fall and I am sure she has missed bossing people around.

"Yo," Javier says, when our savory pies and snacks are finally finished baking and we're chomping on our cheese straws. "These things are gooood."

"Mm-hm," I mumble—talking with your mouth full is a definite no-no in my family, but I don't want Javier to think I'm ignoring him.

"Delicious," Liza says. Since she doesn't have a

crush on Javier, she couldn't care less if she lets a few crumbs fly.

Henry finishes off his last forkful of pot pie and bites into a cheese straw. "Oh yeah," he says, closing his eyes and savoring the salty, tangy flavor, "these are mad good."

We all crack up, especially Javier. He looks extra adorable when he's laughing.

"You know what?" Javier asks when he catches his breath. "I think ours was the best table. We make a great team, don't you think?" He holds his hands up, and the four of us high-five all around.

"Yeah, we do," I say, my mouth finally free of cheese straw. "We make a mad good team."

CHAPTER 16
Liza

Every Sunday morning from ten to ten thirty my dad calls to talk to me and Cole. He used to call it our "weekly phone date," but that sounded seriously weird (and dorky), so I made him stop last year. It's not like he and Cole have much to talk about—construction vehicles mostly—because Cole is not so great at a two-way conversation at this point, so Dad spends most of the time asking me questions about school and my friends and what I did that week. One time he actually asked me if I liked any boys, but I yelled, "Dad!!!" into the phone so violently that he hasn't tried it again.

Lately, my dad and I have been talking a lot about the party on our Sunday calls. Mostly he wants to make sure that Nana isn't driving me *too* crazy with all of her planning. I think he feels guilty that I'm the one who has to deal with her . . . well . . . Nana-ness, since I'm here and he's three thousand miles away. So far I've been assuring him that I can handle it. But yesterday's cooking class made me realize that if there's any chance of this party bringing my parents back together, it's not going to happen while they're on opposite coasts. And if getting them face-to-face before the big, dreaded day means telling my dad that Nana's control freakishness has gotten completely out of control, then that's what I'll have to do. It's not exactly lying, right? And even if it is, it's all for a good cause—my new Big Idea: Operation Reconciliation.

When the phone rings, Cole insists on being the

one to answer, even though he hasn't entirely figured out how phones work yet. Of course, it rings five times before he pushes the right button to actually answer the call. Mom puts it on speakerphone, since Cole doesn't get the whole holding-it-up-to-your-ear thing, but as soon as she does he turns it off. I turn it back on and he turns it off again, giggling up a storm. This goes on for ages, and meanwhile poor Dad is on the other end yelling out, "Cole? Buddy? Is anyone there? Liza? Jackie?" Finally I get fed up and grab the phone. Cole howls, but I don't care—enough is enough and I have big plans for this call.

I peel Cole's sticky hands off my arm and hold the phone out of his reach. "You can talk to Daddy when I'm done," I say. I get up and head for my room, away from his wailing and, more importantly, away from my mom's radar. No way can I have her guessing what I am trying to do, it would ruin everything. This has to seem like *fate*, or something.

"Hi, Dad," I say, closing my door and turning on

music so Mom and Cole can't hear me. Not that it matters much anyway, Cole is still fussing that I took the phone away from him. "Sorry about that."

"That's okay, kiddo. Your brother's just being two and half. Little kids get a kick out of pushing buttons and seeing what happens. It wasn't so long ago that you did stuff like that too."

"Maybe," I say, "but there's no way I was as annoying as Cole."

"You also didn't have a dad who only talked to you out of a little box."

Mr. Mac would call that a "perfect segue"—a seamless transition from one subject to another.

"Yeah," I sigh, just a little dramatically, "I actually wish you were here in person right now."

"What's up, Lize?" my dad asks, sounding concerned. "Is everything okay?"

"Well, I'm just a little stressed out."

"About the party?"

"I guess," I sigh again, getting ready to bring out

the big guns. I'm not Nana Silver's granddaughter for nothing!

My dad exhales loudly into the phone. "What's Nana up to now?"

I pick up the brochure from the super ridiculous party space Nana went nuts over. "Well, she's been putting a lot of pressure on me to have the party at this really fancy place that's a gazillion miles away from Brooklyn, and I'm pretty sure she's hiring the New York Philharmonic to do the music, even though I told her I'd rather have a DJ." Okay, so maybe I'm exaggerating a bit—it's for a good cause, right?

"I thought you said Nana was keeping herself under control," Dad says. "Last time we spoke it sounded like she was willing to compromise."

"Well, she's not," I say, hoping I sound more wounded than bratty, "and I just really wish you were here so I wouldn't have to do this alone." I can almost hear my dad's heart fall to his kitchen floor with a splat.

"What about your mom, Lize, can she try to talk to Nana?"

"Dad, you know Mom's trying to stay out of the whole party thing. She doesn't want to 'overstep' or something. Plus, she says she still has nightmares about Nana Silver 'helping' her plan your wedding."

"Yep, that's true enough," my dad says with a sort of sad chuckle. I think he's starting to break down. "Don't worry, Liza Lou, as soon as I hang up with you guys, I'll give her a call and let her know that she's out of bounds. I'll also *gently* remind her that the party is for *you*, not her."

"But *Daddy*," I whine. I probably sound like I'm five, but calling my father "Daddy" turns him to mush. "Couldn't you just come to New York a week early? That way if Nana's party ends up over the top, at least you'll be here to help tone it down. Come on, Daddy—please?"

I can hear my Dad clicking away on his keyboard. "Well, I'll take a look at my calendar, Lize. I'm not all that excited about tangling with Nana Silver, and I am not sure how much I could help at that point—I mean, won't the damage have been done? But, of course, it would be great to spend some extra time with you and Cole. And your mom and I could discuss a few things in person."

Bingo. He wants to talk to Mom in person! "That would be great, Dad! I feel less stressed out already. Can you book your tickets now?"

"Now?"

"Please, Daddy?" Clearly, I have no shame.

My dad sighs. "Okay, sure, sweetheart. As soon as I hang up the phone."

"Promise?" He's said this kind of thing before.

"Promise. Now how about you give your little brother back the phone? He's not still crying, is he?"

I open my door and there's Cole on the couch, shoving "his" phone—it's really my mom's old one—into his mouth and gnawing on the buttons. Like I said, he doesn't entirely get how to use a phone just yet.

"Wanna talk to Daddy?" I ask, heading over to the couch. I take the dripping old phone out of his mouth and toss it onto the coffee table. Cole grabs for the real phone in my hand, but I yank it away just in time. "Here, I'll show you." I press the speakerphone button. "Now talk."

"Talk!" Cole squawks, picking up the phone with both hands and pressing it to his face.

"What?" I hear my father's muffled voice on the other end. "Cole-Man, is that you?"

I decide to let Mom sort things out this time and head back to my room, practically skipping. I've got a whole week of whirlwind romance and family bonding to plan!

CHAPTER 17
Liza

It's rainy and freezing today, but according to the Clinton Middle School calendar, spring is right around the corner. The Spring Clubs and Teams Fair is going on this afternoon right after school. Lillian and I are waiting at my locker for Frankie, who's the main reason we're even going to the fair. For the past few weeks she's been talking about joining the track team—even though when we played soccer in fourth and fifth grade she was always making up excuses to get out of running sprints at practice. Don't get me wrong, Frankie's a decent athlete, but it's been a while since she's shown any interest in getting sweaty on a regular basis.

We decide that Frankie has either been abducted by aliens or ditched us and gone straight to the fair. Part of me is hoping it's the aliens, because the thought of three entire months of Frankie-less afternoons is seriously depressing. When I text Frankie asking where she is, though, her reply is definitely coming from the first floor gym and not from outer space.

Sorry L! I wanted to beat the crowds.

The Clubs and Teams fairs aren't exactly sold-out stadium shows, so I'm not sure what crowds Frankie is hoping to beat, but Lillian and I grab our stuff and head down to see what's going on.

With Nana expecting me to drop everything to check out "venues" and approve (sort of) invitations every other day, I don't really have time for any extracurriculars other than the Green Club, which Frankie and I have been doing since sixth grade. I've been trying to convince Lillian to join the Green Club too, but she says clubs and teams are Katie's thing. Plus, since she doesn't get perfect grades, her parents think cooking class is enough of a distraction from homework. On the way down to the gym I explain to her that the best thing about Green Club—other than protecting the planet, obviously—is that we can work on our projects during the actual school day, like watering the garden beds during study hall, or helping with the recycling at lunch.

I'm pretty sure I've sold Lillian on saving the Earth, when Mr. Mac swoops over to us as soon as we enter the gym.

"Lillian Wong!" he says, as if they're long lost friends. "I was hoping you'd show up."

Lillian looks at me, totally confused.

"And good afternoon to you, too, Liza," Mr. Mac

says. "I don't mean to imply that I *wasn't* hoping *you'd* show up. It's just that there are some students I really think Lillian should meet."

I'm as confused as Lillian, but I've had enough classes with him to know that this kind of thing is classic Mr. Mac. I scan the room for Frankie, who would normally have rushed right over to join us the second she saw us talking to her teacher crush. The Green Club booth is just a few tables down from the door, and she's not there. I look over toward the bleachers where all the sports teams are set up and spot Frankie's purple leopard-print backpack surrounded by a sea of Clinton Cougars track jackets. She was right—there does seem to be a crowd around all the team tables. I had no idea. I try to catch Frankie's eye, but she's talking to the gym teacher, Tanya, who is also the track-team coach. If I were Frankie, I'd be pretty terrified about a coach who's been known to give her entire class a pop quiz because she caught one kid chewing gum, but

Frankie doesn't even look nervous—and she hasn't noticed that Mr. Mac is standing here chatting with Lillian and me.

Mr. Mac leans back against the edge of the Drama Club table and crosses his arms. "Ever heard of the Poster Club?" he asks Lillian.

Lillian looks at me, but I just shrug—I skimmed the handout listing all the clubs, but I don't remember that one. "I don't think so," Lillian says.

Mr. Mac smiles. "That's because this is the Poster Club's inaugural semester." When other teachers use words like "inaugural" instead of just saying "first" it's annoying, but for some reason Mr. Mac can get away with it.

"Oh," says Lillian. "So what does the club do?"

"I'm glad you asked!" Mr. Mac extends his arm like a restaurant host offering to lead you to your table. "Allow me to show you."

Lillian gives me a "What am I getting into?" look, and Mr. Mac catches it.

"You're welcome to join us, of course, Liza," he says, doing the maître-d' thing again. "There's certainly room for more members." Thanks for the vote of confidence, Mr. Mac.

"That's okay, I'm kind of busy after school these days," I say. Lillian looks a little nervous, so I add, "But I might as well check it out anyway, since you've made it sound so mysterious."

"I like your spirit of curiosity and adventure. Right this way, girls!"

It turns out the Poster Club is exactly what it sounds like—a club for designing and making posters for school events like dances, games, bake sales, and that kind of thing. Mr. Mac says he was tired of seeing "uninspired" posters around the halls that looked like no one put any time or effort into making them. He actually got the idea for the Poster Club when he handed out the flyers for the Clubs and Teams Fair to his homeroom. He says he thought of all of the great social studies projects his students have made and said to himself, "We can do better!" So, he started the Poster Club *today*, and he's been walking around the fair trying to convince all of the good artists, like Lillian, to join. Needless to say, he did not make a beeline for me.

While Lillian is being introduced to some eighth graders in the Poster Club, I look over at the track team table for Frankie. I can't believe she's missing all of this quality time with Mr. Mac. The Frankie I know would have been over here signing up the minute she found out he's the club's faculty advisor, even though she's probably never given the posters in the hallway a second thought. Finally, Frankie catches my eye. I wave and point to the Green Club table. Even though we've been in the club since the fall, we're supposed to put our names on the list again so they know how many spots are open for new members.

Frankie does that universal hand gesture for writing your name. "Just sign me up," she mouths from across the room. This should be good news— at least she's not totally dropping Green Club for track. But somehow I have the feeling I'll be weeding the planters and sorting the bottles and cans solo this spring.

CHAPTER 18

Liza

If I did not love my friends with all my heart, I might just want to kill them right now.

Cooking class is supposed to be all for one and one for all. But lately when we're at the studio, Frankie and Lillian spend the entire time obsessing over how to get Tristan and Javier to talk to them, instead of hanging out with me. And if that weren't bad enough, the whole thing with Chef complimenting my mom and asking her to help out during class all the time still gets me a little worried. Even Cole has Angelica to play with every week. What's left for me?

Chef Antonio waves his arms and summons us to the work area. And when I say he waves, I mean he really waves. He makes big swooping motions with his arms and calls out, "*Vamanos, vamanos!* Come, *mis amigos*, the clock is ticking. Let's get our party started!"

Most of us make our way to the tables, following directions, but Frankie and Lillian hang back by the door waiting to see where the boys will sit. I catch Lillian's eye, and she seems to notice for the first time that I'm standing all by myself. She whispers something to Frankie, and they head toward me. Finally, some loyalty.

Chef rubs his hands together. "Ah, we have so many treats in store today. So many, *mi gente*, that I will need to call upon my favorite consultant to help us so we can explore as many *sabrosos*, sweets, from different parts of this country. *Bueno, bueno.*"

Surprise, surprise. I think we can all guess who his favorite consultant might be. Dr. Wong looks slightly irritated, because I'm guessing she considers herself consultant-worthy too, even if today's class is about American snacks.

Chef gestures to the tables. "Everyone will get to do everything, but we will have to split up into groups and work at different tables again and then switch around when the time comes. On the menu today, we have unique cookies that all are greedy for space and need to be made with care. *Sí?* So, we will have whoopie pies over here"—he points to the table at his left—"black-and-white cookies over there"—and then to the one on the right—"and half-moon pies in the middle." He gives my mother a big grin. "Señora Jackie is the guide for the half-moon pies, since they are a Southern specialty, just like she is!"

Oh boy. I don't even have to look at Frankie and Lillian to know that they're exchanging significant glances. I steer them toward the whoopie pies. I don't think I really know what they are (any relation to whoopie cushion? If you sit down at Frankie's house, there's at least a 50 percent chance you'll land on one of those), but I'm in no mood to face my mother, at least not yet.

As it shakes out, we're at the whoopee-pie table with Henry, who smiles at us in his usual calm, sweet way even though he's still in midconversation with Dr. Wong. They're debating the qualities of baking powder and baking soda, as she takes her place at the black-and-white cookie station with Javier, Tristan, and Errol. Frankie's mom and the Newlyweds are with my mom at her table. Theresa announces to anyone listening that Mom manages to turn all of her messes into something magical. Sad, but true.

According to the clipboard holding our recipe, whoopie pies are two round discs of cake with frosting sandwiched between them. No connection to rubber prank toys that make farting noises at all. Things are looking up.

Chef chuckles as he tells us that the whoopie pie is also called a devil dog, a BFO (for Big Fat Oreo), a bob (huh?), or a gob—but only in Pittsburgh. Bizarre.

"In Maine," Chef continues, "the whoopie pie is so famous, it was made the official state treat! We will never really know, of course, who invented the whoopie pie, but food historians—yes, they actually exist!—believe they first appeared when nineteenth-century Amish farm women decided to use leftover batter to make small cakes for *sus maridos*—their husbands—to eat in the fields for lunch. Wherever they came from, I'm very glad they did, because they are *muy delicioso* as you will soon see! So let's make some whoopies!"

Lillian steals a glance at Javier every time Chef makes a lame joke. Sometimes he catches her looking and rolls his eyes in that my-dad-is-so-embarrassing way. I'm glad they're getting to be friends, and even more glad that Lillian isn't as over-the-top as Frankie. I love Franks, but sometimes it's hard to watch her act the way she acts when she has a massive crush.

As we work on our batter—Henry is making gingerbread whoopie pies, but Frankie, Lillian, and I chose chocolate—I whisper to them that the plan for Operation Reconciliation is underway. I tell them how Dad is coming out early for some QT, and now I just need to figure out what sorts of things we should do that will remind him and my mom how much better we are as a family of four, rather than three plus one.

"What about the Bronx Zoo or a carriage ride in Central Park?" Lillian says while she carefully measures out our ingredients. "Or the Statue of Liberty? I want to take my cousins there when they come out for spring break."

I shake my head. "Nothing too ambitious or overwhelming for Cole. All thoughts of romance will fly out the window if he spends all day having tantrums." Our batter is almost done, and yet I keep pressing the beat button on the super-duper mixer. I need the sound to mask our conversation. "And besides," I add, "even though Dad's out in LA now, my parents lived here for years—they've already done all of that touristy stuff." Actually, I've lived in New York City my entire life and

I've never been to the Statue of Liberty or taken a carriage ride in the park. But they must have, right?

Frankie scrapes down the sides of the bowl so all the batter gets mixed in. "Okay, how about painting pottery on Smith Street? Or ice-skating in Prospect Park? That's like the perfect wholesome family activity."

Henry peers at us over the top of his glasses. "Did I hear you say you girls are going ice-skating in Prospect Park? Beautiful new rink. Love that place!" I give him a nervous smile and glance over at my mom. If she hears us plotting, Operation Reconciliation will be over before my dad even gets here.

"Yeah, we already went with school," I say, not really wanting to keep the conversation going. "Really really long lines, but it was super nice." I kick her under the table. Hasn't she ever heard of whispering?

"Oops! Sorry." She shrugs, and she actually looks like she means it. But still, we're supposed to be talking about a *secret* plan.

We drop big round tablespoons of dough onto

baking trays covered in parchment paper to prevent sticking. While our whoopie pies are baking, we make the frosting by beating powdered sugar and butter until it's fluffy, sweet, and creamy. Henry adds some cinnamon to his, to go with the gingerbread, but we stick with the basics. Frankie and I have always been frosting freaks, but while Lillian has been sampling from our bowl as much as I have, Frankie hasn't had a single lick. She keeps coming up with reasons to borrow things from Tristan's table, like measuring spoons, or extra butter (even though we have loads). Tristan doesn't react all that much when Frankie stops by—I guess by now her behavior seems normal—but that doesn't stop Frankie from trying.

While we wait for the whoopie pies to cool so we can ice them (with whatever we haven't eaten), we move to the black-and-white cookie table.

"Hey, girls, nice to see you!" Theresa says—she's checking out the black-and-whites while her pies cool too. "I could eat my weight in these things, couldn't you?" I love Frankie's mom, but if she sticks around, when will we finish plotting my perfect week of family togetherness?

Chef Antonio pops up like a Jack-in-the-Box to get us started on the black-and-whites. "*Señoritas,* these are famous New York cookies—remember Jerry Seinfeld?"

Frankie's mom laughs, but I have no idea what Chef is talking about. Frankie and Lillian look as confused as I am, so I decide it's a generation gap thing. "*Bueno,*" Chef continues, "these are cookies, not cakes, so the dough will be stiffer and less runny. We use buttermilk, so they will be *ricos y sabrosos*— rich and tasty. Also, these bambinos must be big and round, with plenty of room to split them down the middle and fill in one side *blanco* and one side *negro.* And for that, we will use fondant, not regular icing. Fondant, *mis amigos, comprenden?* Here we go!"

We all start pouring in ingredients, because by now we're old hands at this baking thing. Well, maybe not all of us. Theresa misses the bowl as she's sifting the flour and winds up leaving little mounds of powder all over the table. She tries to scoop it all back into her bowl, but accidentally dumps her reading glasses in there too. While she's off washing them in the sink, I try to ask Frankie and Lillian for more family fun ideas, but they're only half paying attention. Tristan and Javier are having a mixing contest over at their table, and watching that is apparently way more interesting. By the time Theresa gets back, our cookies are in the oven and we're starting on the icing—I mean fondant.

Frankie stirs our confectioners' sugar, corn syrup, lemon juice, vanilla, and very hot water in a small bowl until it's smooth. She's really focused on smooshing out any little sugar lumps. Lately, everything Frankie does needs to be absolutely perfect. "Franks," I murmur, trying again. "Seriously, what else can I plan for my mom and dad?"

"Well, hmm," she pushes her hair behind her ear and wrinkles her brow like she does when she's really thinking. I feel better already. "What makes my parents happy is when we're all together. My mom says it all the time, she just loves it when we're all in the same place. It doesn't really matter what we're doing, just that we're all doing it. You know?" She looks over at her mom and Lillian as they struggle to smooth the lumps in Theresa's fondant. I'm guessing her water wasn't actually hot—Chef says that's the trick—but who knows.

Frankie sighs and leans forward. "What if you did all the normal things that your dad is probably missing? Go wherever you always went, show him the everyday things that make you guys you? You could even make a slideshow of photos on your computer and act like you're just catching him up, but then really try to show him everything he's missing out on." She gives the fondant another stir and then shrugs. "Or you could just lock all four of you in the apartment for the week and tell your mom and dad they can't leave until they're engaged again."

"Ha-ha," I say, giving Frankie a shove.

We divide the fondant into two bowls, adding

cocoa powder to one to make it black while leaving the other one just vanilla. When the cookies come out of the oven, we flip them over to ice the flatter side. Lillian manages to make her fondant halves perfectly even, a razor-sharp straight line separating the black from the white. Frankie's and mine are more wobbly-looking, but still pretty good. Poor Theresa's look like one of Cole's finger paintings, with the colors blurring together—more gray than anything else. First she seems irritated and frustrated, kind of hissing at them under her breath. Then, despite the mess, she just laughs and calls them melting pot cookies (because, as we all learned in Mr. Mac's class last semester, when it comes to cultures and flavors, New York is like a melting pot).

Now that I'm in a better mood, I think I can handle Mom's half-moon pies. I know I've seen her make them before, but not in a long time. They're different from today's other treats because they are actually made with pie crust and filling, so they truly are mini pies.

"Last but not least, huh?" my mom says as Frankie, Lillian, and I gather around her table. It looks like everyone else has made theirs.

She tells us about growing up smelling these little pies baking all the time, like after school, or on Saturday mornings. When there was overripe fruit, her mother or grandmother would whip some up so she'd have a surprise in her lunchbox. I've always loved Mom's stories, and now that Operation Reconciliation is getting underway, I can relax a little and enjoy them again.

Mom points to a big bowl of fruit and tells us to chop up whatever we like. Since we're the final group, there are just a few apples and pears left, so we grab those and get started. When we're finished slicing and dicing, we cook the fruit on the stove with a sprinkle of sugar and cinnamon and watch it soften. I tell Lillian about Frankie's idea while we stir.

"So, I'll just remind my dad—over and over—about how great our normal family life used to be," I explain. "And then at some point, he'll suddenly realize all that he's missing. Simple, yet elegant, right?" Lillian looks at Frankie and then back at me.

"Yeah, definitely," she says, sounding less than convinced. I was expecting her to be more positive about my plan, but I decide that it's just that her family isn't into "togetherness" the way Frankie's is. I can't exactly picture Dr. Wong, Lillian, Katie, and the other Dr. Wong all hanging out on a couch together watching TV—and they definitely don't do pizza night.

When our fruit is ready, we cut circles in our dough and plop the warm mush in the center. Some fruit oozes out of my pie when I fold over the edges, but I wipe it off with my finger and sneak a taste. Yum. Problem solved.

Mom watches carefully as we fry our pies in vegetable oil, because it's easy to get burned. Actually, the popping, sizzling oil does sting me a couple of times, but who cares? As I place my little pies on paper towels and watch the oil soak in, I picture making them for Dad as we enjoy a family breakfast. And that makes Nana Silver, the party, and a few pops of oil totally worth it.

CHAPTER 19
Liza

"Should we feel guilty sitting here eating while Frankie's out there running?" Lillian asks. We're munching on the seriously delicious leftovers from whatever Dr. Wong made for dinner last night, and attempting to do our homework while Frankie is at the first official day of track team training. Apparently, before you even try out for the team, you have to do two whole weeks of training, which means that our Frankie-less afternoons have started even sooner than I expected.

"Nope," I say, spooning some wide, flat noodles onto my plate. "More for us."

I'm trying to be a supportive friend and "keep an open mind," as my mom would say, about Frankie's new obsession with track and raw vegetables. But it's hard to watch your best friend suddenly morph into someone you don't recognize.

Lillian pours us each a glass of iced tea that's been brewing on the counter. It tastes like flowers, in the absolute best way. "Do you think Frankie will make the team?"

I shrug, smelling and tasting the incredible tea all at once. "You know Frankie—when she gets an idea into her head, she just goes for it."

"Yeah," Lillian says with a sigh, "it would be nice if that were contagious."

I slurp down my final noodle and push my plate away. "Don't tell me you wanted to join the track team too. I thought that was Katie's deal."

"Ha! No way." Lillian laughs. "But, I don't know,

I wish I could be more like Frankie around . . . you know . . ."

"Boys? As in Tristan?"

Lillian nods. "It's like she's not even nervous around him. And he's in high school!"

"But don't you think Frankie sometimes acts, I don't know, a little *too* confident around him?" I ask. "You know, talking to him nonstop, never taking a breath, hitting him on the shoulder whenever *she* says something funny . . ."

"Maybe, but at least she doesn't start blushing every time he's even remotely nearby," Lillian says, absently twirling a noodle around one of her chopsticks. "Do you think Javier even knows I exist?"

"Of course, Lils!" I'm not sure *I've* ever called her Lils before, but I kind of like it. "Javier's not exactly a major talker, but I'd say he definitely likes you at least as a friend."

"So what do I do if I want him to like me as more than a friend?"

"I'm not really an expert, but I don't think the Francesca Caputo method is the way to go with Javier. If you went full-Frankie on him, I'm pretty sure he'd spend the rest of our cooking classes hiding out in the corner with my brother."

Lillian and I both crack up at the thought of Javier dancing and playing patty-cake with Cole and Angelica. Of course, perfect Katie picks the exact moment when we're laughing like dorks to float in through the kitchen door. She's in her workout gear, as usual, chugging—in the most elegant way possible—from a bottle of spring water. For someone who plays three sports, you'd think she'd have discovered refillable water bottles by now. If she went to Clinton, I'd sign her up for the Green Club's Reduce, Reuse, Recycle workshop ASAP.

"Whew!" Katie sighs, tossing her empty bottle into the sink. "Today's practice was killer. Coach Ryan was clearly in a mood." I've heard from Lillian that Katie always carries on about the strictness of the high school coach. I guess she thinks it makes her accomplishments all the more superior. She looks from Lillian and me to the bowls of leftovers and our practically licked-clean plates.

"You must be starving," Lillian says, pushing the noodles across the table toward Katie. "There's still a lot left—have some."

Katie shakes her head and flashes a big photo-worthy smile. "I can hold out until dinner, thanks. But I hope you two enjoyed your feast."

Lillian rolls her eyes. "It was just a snack—we've been working since we got home from school and you know dinner's not till seven, at least. Just take some already."

"No time, Lillian. These books won't crack themselves, as Mama likes to say. I'll just grab a couple of grapes . . . unless you girls are still hungry. "

I give Lillian a look. If my mom were here, she'd say Katie's "a piece of work," just like Nana Silver. The thought of Nana and Katie together makes me laugh—if I end up inviting the entire Wong family to my not-mitzvah, I'll definitely have to sit them at a table together so they can try to out-snob each other.

Katie pulls one giant textbook after another out of her bag and piles them up on the table, just in case we've forgotten that she takes a hundred advanced classes. "Oh," she says, when the pile is at least five books high, "I almost forgot—I saw your friend Frankie at the track. It looked like she was working really hard. I'm impressed."

I'd forgotten that the middle and high schools share a track. So of course Katie would see Frankie.

"Today was the first day of preseason training. Do you think she's good enough to make the team?" I ask, knowing that no matter what she says, part of me will be happy and the other part, well, not so much.

"I didn't spend my entire practice assessing the middle school hopefuls," Katie says, taking the two biggest books off the pile and tucking them under her arm, "but I did notice her keeping up with the pack. That's not an easy feat for someone who hasn't been in training. And she seemed pretty determined, which is something coaches look for."

"That's good," I say, glancing at Lillian, "I guess."

Lillian shrugs. "Good for Frankie. Lonely for us."

With her free hand, Katie digs a doodle-free notebook out of her backpack. "You know, Lillian, it wouldn't hurt you to try out for an athletic team too. It's not like you have a packed schedule or anything."

"Actually," Lillian says, "I just joined the Clinton Poster Club. So I'll be pretty busy this spring."

"Right," Katie says, giving us one of her half smiles. "Sounds exhausting."

With the bunch of grapes balanced delicately on her pile, Katie waltzes out of the room. Perfect is definitely *not* the word I'd use for her right now!

CHAPTER 20
Frankie

What's that expression about a body at rest staying at rest? Mom likes to say it when The Goons are parked, well, anywhere: their beds, the couch, the floor, the kitchen chairs. Sprawled out, legs and arms flopped all over the place, no sense that other people might need to get by or exist in the same space, they do it all the time. As annoying as they are, crashing through the house leaving a trail of destruction in their wake, The Goons seem to irritate Mom more at the opposite end of their very limited spectrum—teenage boy limbs draped everywhere. So she claps at them in her second-grade teacher way, proclaiming something about bodies staying at rest and urging them to remove themselves promptly and go do "something productive." Of course, I find them unbearable in either state, but that's just me.

Right now, my own body is screaming to be at rest. The first day of training for the track team was pretty killer and maybe not quite as cool as I thought it would be. I mean, since I've essentially been running since right after I learned to walk, honestly, how hard could it be? Instead, we do long laps where my lungs don't ever fill with the necessary oxygen, and then short sprints where my legs never seem to extend far enough that my thighs will stop screaming in pain. I'm panting like Rocco on a hot day and my hair is everywhere I don't want it to be—strands sticking to my neck, pasted to my cheeks, poking in my eyes—even though it started out crammed into a fat pink elastic. So much for my bouncy, effortless jog!

I huff and puff all the way home and miraculously make it to my room without being assaulted by any member of my family. I can hear them, stomping around in the kitchen as Dad finishes dinner, yelling over one another to be heard, but somehow nobody notices me creeping in. Who am I kidding? I was hardly creeping, more like *trudging* or maybe even *lumbering* thanks to my total exhaustion. (Mr. Mac would be seriously impressed with my vocabulary. But do I even care anymore?) However you describe it, I'm safe in my own little space where I can relax for a second before I take off these sweaty clothes and get in the shower . . .

BANG BANG BANG.

The next thing I know, there's an ear-splitting crashing noise and a blazing overhead light blasts into my eyes. Did I fall asleep? Nicky is standing in the middle of the room with his hands on his hips like a mini version of Mom.

"Frankie! Mom says to come now. We've been calling you forever and she was starting to get worried that there was something wrong with you." He peers at me from above, sizing me up. "Is there something wrong with you? You look weird."

"No," I mumble, "I'm fine. Now get out."

"Mom, she's okay," he hollers, loud enough to be heard downstairs. "Except she's all sweaty-looking and mean!"

I hear my mom ask him if she needs to come up to check on me.

I stagger up, not wanting her to think I'm sick. "I'm totally fine. And I'm not mean. You just have no business in my room, that's all. Tell her I'm coming right now!"

Nicky plows down the stairs ahead of me, while I follow slowly. I never fall asleep during the day, and I have no memory of deciding to take a nap, anyway. That just doesn't happen to me. Maybe that is what people mean by power napping? Does Katie power nap? Is that how she crams so much into one day without getting wiped out? But I don't feel "powerful" or even energized. I just feel disgusting.

Of course, it's a night when every single Caputo is home, so when I get to the table, all five of them look up at me. If I look even half as bad as I feel, I'm not a pretty sight. From the expressions on my family's faces, they clearly agree. Oh well.

"You okay, bella?" my mom asks. "You look tired."

Before I can answer, The Goons start snickering. "Stop it, boys," Mom says. "Francesca is working very hard, give her a break." I appreciate her effort, but my obnoxious brothers just keep making stupid comments about dangling a cannoli on a stick in front of my face when I'm running—like a tastier, more tempting carrot—or putting a plate of risotto at the finish line.

"Cut it out now, boys," Dad says in his I-mean-business voice, so The Goons just sort of shrug and start shoveling food onto their plates and then into their gaping mouths, pretty much simultaneously.

Sometimes with the same fork. Revolting.

As Dad passes the steaming pan to me, while still keeping an eye on the human garbage disposals, I have to admit: his lasagna looks amazing. Layers of pasta and slices of eggplant, chopped peppers, ground beef, tomato sauce, spices, and—of course—cheese. I would so love to slice off a piece as big as my plate and dive in. Instead, I force myself to focus on Katie and her discipline. Katie and her ambition to succeed. Katie and her fruit and tea and her perfect grades and her perfect track team medals. I can do that too, can't I? I can be the Frankie who's determined and centered and healthy, not the Frankie who's driven by immediate gratification, no matter how much that gratification is smothered in melted cheese. I can be the Frankie who people like Katie and Tristan actually take seriously.

Yep. That's what I'm talking about. I can see it now. Dream it, be it.

Taking just a sliver of lasagna, I reach for the

spinach salad and pile my plate high with pine-nut sprinkled dark leafy greens—the healthiest kind, according to a nutrition book someone left on the bench in the locker room this afternoon. Spinach makes you strong, right? That's what Popeye says, anyway, and with some of my dad's homemade dressing, it's actually quite tasty.

Now that they've nearly finished with stuffing their faces, The Goons are taking turns imitating a supposedly certifiable chemistry teacher they both had, and Nicky is literally spitting out his food with hysterics. But do I throw a fit and tell them off? Do I roll my eyes and sigh at their stupidity? No, not this Frankie. Instead I'm determined to maintain my composure. Even my parents are laughing—but not me. I keep my head down and focus on my breathing until the Joey and Leo comedy routine ends.

With dinner finally over, the boys disappear as usual. Apparently, my Nonna had dropped off some amaretti cookies earlier today, and my brothers each grab a fistful before they take off.

Since Dad cooks, Mom's on cleanup. I start to help her clear the table, but she kisses my nose and waves me upstairs. "Go take a shower and get ready for school tomorrow. You need sleep, Francesca, you look wiped out."

Great. Even my mom thinks I look like crap. I follow her instructions, though. Once I'm clean and refreshed, I will be ready to take on my humanities homework—and maybe some extra credit math problems to get my grade up a bit more. After that, who knows? I might even memorize a few global capitals so I have a shot at making the Model UN in a couple of years, like Katie.

Yes, I'm so totally going to do all of that— right after I spread out on my soft, warm, strawberry-covered comforter for a minute or two. Just a minute . . . or two . . .

CHAPTER 21
Liza

I know it's scientifically impossible and all that, but I could swear that time literally slows down at the end of eighth period, so that the last ten minutes actually take at least twenty. Even though humanities is one of my favorite classes, by the end of the period— which is also the end of the school day—I usually find myself watching those last endless minutes tick down until the bell rings.

Not today though. For the first time all year—

maybe ever—I wish those clock hands would move even slower. After school Nana's taking me shopping for a dress, and I'm dreading it even more than our tour of possible party spaces or our visit to the letterpress studio. Don't get me wrong, I like going shopping (not as much as Frankie, but she's obsessed), I just can't imagine a dress existing in this universe that Nana Silver and I will agree on. The only good thing about this shopping trip is that Frankie and Lillian are coming along for moral support—and they've promised to come to my rescue if Nana tries to make me look like the newest Disney princess (even though a half-Jewish, half–African American princess would be pretty cool).

When the bell *finally* rings, I take my time organizing my notebook and pause to redo my ponytail a few times while looking at my reflection in the window. I'm the last one out of the room, and when I get to my locker, Frankie and Lillian are already there waiting.

"What took you so long?" Frankie asks. "I could have run around the track three times by now." Frankie's skipping preseason track for this afternoon's adventure, and this is at least the fifth time she's brought it up since lunch. She actually jogged up and down the stairs between classes to make up for missing the workout.

"I'm not exactly in a hurry to see myself in all those poofy, frilly dresses that Nana picks out," I say. "Even *I* think running around the track sounds like the better option."

"Come on, Liza, it'll be fun," Lillian says. "If we were shopping with my grandmother, you'd end up with one of those old-fashioned high-necked Chinese dresses that practically choke you to death."

I grab my backpack and jacket and slam my locker shut. "I have a feeling I'd rather wear one of those than anything Nana's got in mind."

"Where are we going, anyway?" Frankie asks as we head toward the main stairway.

"I have no idea," I say, "I was afraid to ask. Probably wherever Cinderella would shop if she lived in New York."

Outside, Nana is waiting for us in a taxi, right in front of school just like last time. As soon as she sees us, she makes the driver honk the horn, even though it's the only taxi on the block and we're already walking directly toward it. When the three of us reach the cab, Nana gets out and gives me a quick hug and kiss. Frankie leans in to hug her next, but Nana takes Frankie's face in her hands instead.

"Francesca," she says, beaming at Frankie as if she'd just earned a scholarship to Harvard. "Look at you!" Nana lets go of Frankie's cheeks and steps back a little, giving us all more space to admire her. "So tall! And that gorgeous Mediterranean skin."

Instead of turning as red as my grandmother's lipstick, Frankie just smiles. She's used to Nana and is great at talking to adults, period. "Hi, Mrs. Silver. It's so nice to see you. I hope you don't mind us tagging along."

Nana waves Frankie's politeness away like it's a pesky fly. "Please, Francesca, call me Adele. I've known you since you were this high." She reaches her hand down to just above her knee, which is an exaggeration, but I'm not about to call her on it.

"And who is this lovely young lady?" Nana asks, turning to Lillian.

"This is Lillian, Nana," I say, putting my arm around Lillian's shoulders. "She moved here from San Francisco in September—but Frankie and I have no idea how we ever survived without her."

"Nice to meet you, Mrs. Silver," Lillian says, holding her hand out in this very stiff and formal way.

Instead of shaking, Nana pulls Lillian in for a hug and an air-kiss. "It's Adele to you, too, sweetheart. Look at that glossy hair and delicate bone structure. Fabulous! My goodness. Well, welcome to the East Coast."

Lillian's family doesn't do a lot of hugging, and the way she talks about her other relatives, I get the feeling they don't either. From the look on Lillian's face right now, I'm guessing she's never met anyone like Nana Silver before.

"So, girls, now that we're all old friends, how about we get this show on the road and do some shopping?" Nana says, ushering the three of us into the back of the taxi and settling herself into the passenger's seat.

"To Bloomingdale's!" she tells the driver a little too loudly, and then gives him specific instructions about what bridge to take and which avenues will have the least amount of traffic at this hour. I'm sure my grandmother isn't the first micromanaging passenger the guy has ever had to deal with, but I can't help feeling a little sorry for him anyway.

"She's like a real New Yorker!" Lillian whispers into my ear excitedly as the taxi finally pulls away from school.

That's one way of putting it, I think, as Nana compares our taxi driver's GPS directions with the ones on her phone. (When did she learn how to use the map app, anyway?)

When I was younger, I used to love going to Bloomingdale's. My mom hates department stores in general, so we'd only go around the holidays or before special occasions, like my cousin Emma's wedding or Cole's baby naming, which made the place feel sort of magical. Bloomingdale's is always crowded with tourists, and just passing by the perfume section can give you an instant headache, but making the trip into Manhattan to try on pretty clothes once or twice a year was something I looked forward to anyway.

Until now, that is. Even though it's barely March, all of the "nice" dresses in the juniors department have been moved into a special area called Prom Night. When we got off the escalator and Nana brought us here, Frankie, Lillian, and I all looked at each other and I knew we were thinking the same thing.

"No way, Nana, I am *not* getting a prom dress!" I

practically shouted. But the next thing I know, here I am, in a flowery-smelling, peach-colored dressing room, trying on floor-length gowns that are supposed to be worn by actual teenagers to the fanciest event of the year.

Apparently, my grandmother trusts a professional opinion over ours. She's booked a personal shopper to help us find a dress—and not even the same one who's doing the goodie bags. Nicole, our "PS," as she calls herself, keeps telling me how adorable I am and how "delicious" I'm going to look at the party. She could be right—every dress she brings in makes me look like I'm wearing a wedding cake, or the toppings on an ice cream sundae.

Not surprisingly, the poofiest and laciest dresses Nicole shows us are the ones Nana likes best. The more I look like I'm an overgrown four-year-old on my way to a ballet recital, the happier she is. If Frankie and Lillian thought I exaggerated about Nana's taste in party dresses before, I can tell that they're getting the picture now.

While Nana zips me into a shiny tube of lavender satin with a giant cloudlike tutu at the bottom, Frankie whispers something in Nicole's ear and the two of them leave the dressing room together. When they come back, Nicole is carrying a dark-blue dress that's simple, pretty, and entirely poof-less. It's the kind of dress my mom used to wear to magazine parties, when she still went out and did glamorous things like that. It's perfect—and of course Nana hates it.

"Liza, you're the guest of honor at a birthday party, not a funeral," Nana says, fingering the soft, delicate (shine-free) fabric distrustfully, as though it might be covered in a layer of invisible slime.

"It's navy blue, Nana, not black," I correct her. "And I like it so much better than any of the others. At least let me try it on."

Nicole flashes Nana her best PS smile (she's obviously had a lot of practice). "We call this shade midnight blue, and it's a lovely compliment to Liza's mocha skin tones."

I've never thought of my skin color as "mocha" before, but I sort of like it. It sounds a lot nicer than "light brown" or "dark tan," which is how people usually describe me.

"So go ahead, try it on," Nana shrugs. She lays on an overly dramatic, heavy sigh. "Far be it for me to stop you."

As Nicole helps me out of the lavender frill-fest, I look over at Frankie and telepathically say "thank you." I decide to focus on her thumbs-up and Lillian's encouraging smile rather than the annoyed look on Nana's face that I can see reflected in the mirror.

The perfect blue dress actually fits me perfectly too. Nicole straps my feet into a pair of pretty silver sandals that have just the right size heel—a "kitten heel" she calls it—and for a minute I really do feel like Cinderella.

Frankie and Lillian jump up and crowd around me in front of the mirror.

"Oh, Liza," Lillian says, "you look so elegant!"

"You really do, Lize," Frankie says, nodding. "It's just so . . . so totally you."

She takes at least a hundred pictures with her phone as Nicole slowly turns me around so she can get a good look at me and the dress from all sides.

"I have to agree," she says after I've made a full three-sixty rotation. "I think this might be the one."

I take a long look at my reflection in the mirror—the midnight-blue dress, the kitten-heeled shoes, my mocha skin and corkscrew curls—and smile for probably the first time all afternoon. And then I look more carefully at Nana, who is definitely *not* smiling. She sighs, and I know what's coming next.

"I take my granddaughter shopping for a dress to celebrate her most important birthday, and she wants the one that makes her look like she's in mourning."

I shake my head—I have to hold my ground. "Nana, come on. This is a beautiful dress."

"A beautiful dress for a grown woman, maybe." Nana shrugs.

"I thought you said turning thirteen means I *am* a woman."

Nana takes my hand and gives me her best wounded look. "Liza dear, you're becoming a young woman—but you're still my little girl. There must be something else you tried on that you liked."

I look from Frankie to Lillian to Nicole, hoping at least one of them can save me. I can tell they want to help, but what can they do? It's like my grandmother has cast a spell and everyone is suddenly powerless against her.

I gaze at myself in the midnight-blue dress for what I know will be the last time. "Um," I say, my smile long gone, "I guess the pale green one was okay."

Nana lights up. "The pale green was nice, but the lavender brought out the pink in your cheeks." She turns to Nicole. "Don't you agree?"

Nicole shoots me an apologetic look, and then nods.

As my mom would say, Nana Silver strikes again.

CHAPTER 22
Lillian

Chef is clapping and waving his hands around, but I can't take my eyes off my mother. Who would have thought that the proud, stubborn, turn-up-her-nose-at-all-food-not-made-in-her-own-kitchen MeiYin Wong would be this person in front of me—smiling calmly on the outside, but totally excited on the inside about recipes that are as far from Chinese as they can be. According to Chef, we're baking cakes today. For our last class of the session (already?) he wants us to "bake our little hearts out"—and my mother is ready, even though she's never even liked cake.

Today we line up at the long shiny tables where the Newlyweds are chatting about their wedding cake and Ms. Reynolds is going on about what she wants to bake for Liza's party. My mother is so interested that she doesn't notice me slowly moving away from her and closer to Frankie. Unfortunately, Javier is way on the other side of the table near Liza and her mom, but today is not about him. Instead I have to focus on coming up with a plan to rescue Liza's party with Frankie.

Chef has us start with a basic pound cake, which I'm guessing is named for the pounds of butter it seems to need—or the five eggs that must weigh at least a pound. All around the tables are little bowls (Chef calls them "ramekins"—which I think is such a cute word) filled with different things to add to our cakes. After we cream the butter and beat in the other ingredients in the giant red mixers, we get to decide what flavors to add: nutmeg, cinnamon, cardamom, cloves, ginger, colored sugar, or even poppy seeds. There are also bowls of lemons, oranges, limes, and grapefruits for us to "zest," which Chef explains means to shave off tiny pieces of the peel, also called zest, to flavor the pound cake.

Everyone is mixing and matching, which is super fun, and the smell of the citrus fruits is incredible. I look over at my mother, who has somehow become queen of the add-ins and is advising everyone around her which combinations to try. If my hands weren't so sticky from zesting, I'd take a video and send it to my cousin Chloe. She'd never believe this was her Ayi MeiYin.

Frankie's far away from her mom today too, and I can tell she's relieved she doesn't have to watch out for Theresa's "accidents"—or clean up after them. Frankie's not near Tristan either, which is good news for me, since we have things to discuss. Weirdly, it seems like Frankie wants to talk about Liza too.

"Poor Liza," she says as we pour our dough into loaf pans. "She's so miserable about the party, but everyone else can't stop talking about it."

It's true—the whole cooking class seems really interested in the party. Maybe not Nana Silver–level interested, but our three mothers, the Newlyweds, Chef, Henry, and Errol are always coming up with suggestions for the food or the decorations or the music. Of course, now that I've seen Liza's grandmother in action, I realize that none of these opinions really matter. And at this point, Liza looks like she's ready to hide in the oven with the loaf pans just to get away from it all.

As we carefully carry our pound cakes to the oven, Chef asks Javier to help him clear away the ramekins so we can start on the next project: a layer cake. Apparently, you can make all kinds of crazy cakes with a simple layer cake recipe, and I get excited thinking about different shapes and icings and colors.

"*Mis amigos*, we can make a classic birthday cake,

with two or three levels and icing in between each one," Chef explains. "Or imagine little tiny baby cakes baked in our ramekins for one person to savor all to himself," he looks around the room and smiles, "or herself, of course."

"We can dot them with little puffs of whipped cream or decorate with tiny icing flowers. We can make anything with layer cakes, *señoras, señoritas, y señores*—even delicious cupcakes or birthday cakes in the shape of a dinosaur or *un avión*—an airplane!"

Chef moves closer to Liza. "We can even make a cake for a fancy ball," he says, winking at her. Liza forces a smile back, but I can tell she just wants to flee.

Everybody laughs at Chef Antonio's enthusiasm— I think maybe he's purposely being even more Chef-like than usual for our last class—and then starts grabbing whatever they need. Tristan and Javier tell us they're making a rectangle chocolate cake and decorating it like an iPod. I overhear Margo tell Liza they should make a big "thirteen" cake for her party—Liza's too polite to say no, but I'm sure she'd rather be making just about anything else.

"Liza is definitely miserable," I say as Frankie and I start mixing our ingredients. I feel a little guilty that we're paired up and Liza's across the table, but now seems like as good a time as any to bring up my idea. "We should do something to help her."

Frankie rattles the flour sifter just a little too violently and powders herself with a fine pale dust. She shakes herself in a move that reminds me of her pug Rocco and scrunches up her nose. "But if her parents are powerless against Nana Silver, then what can we do?"

I'm trying to figure out how to make a kitten-shaped cake with pointed ears, but then I decide to keep it simple and try some baby cakes. I'm not sure exactly what they are, but the name couldn't be cuter. "Actually, I have an idea," I say, pouring some batter into a ramekin. "What if we threw a more Liza-like not-mitzvah?"

She stops cracking eggs and stares at me. "You mean, like, hijack Nana Silver's party? I love your sense of adventure, but I'm not sure how we'd do that."

Chef scoots by us, encouraging us to hurry along so we can get to the other goodies, and pauses when he gets to my mother.

"*Que lindo*, Mei Yin," he says, and you can tell from his voice that he's genuinely impressed. "So light and fluffy. You are an expert at the batter!"

I can practically feel my mother beaming with pride, and I wonder if she's going to start baking cakes at home, too. For our birthdays, we have longevity noodles, which we get to slurp because its bad luck to cut them or bite them. Maybe she will add in a birthday cake, too? But right now it's time to focus on Liza's birthday.

"What if we somehow threw her the party that she would love, in a comfy, pretty place, with good music, and real-people food, and with everybody that she actually likes?" I say. "We can't stop Nana Silver's party, but maybe we can throw her another one."

Chef scoots along the table again, clapping and encouraging.

"Let's get these in the oven so we can start on the next batch, *mis estudiantes*. We will need to leave time for decorating, because that's where we can all go *loco!*"

Frankie pours her batter into a circular pan—she says she's going to cut it into a heart shape later—and hands it to Chef to put in the oven. "You mean . . . ," she says, when he's definitely too far away to hear, "like an alterna-mitzvah?"

I nod. I guess that's exactly what I mean.

Frankie's eyes get bigger and bigger and she grabs me by the shoulders. "That's GENIUS!"

Henry and my mother look over at us, and I point to the clipboard with the recipe for our next assignment.

They look a little confused, but Henry smiles and

shrugs. "The girl is passionate about her pastry!" he says to my mother.

I want to talk more about the alterna-mitzvah, but Chef starts telling us about shortcake. "This humble little cake is a bit controversial," he explains, "because some people think it should be more biscuit and less cake and some people like it more cake and less biscuit. We are going to make a *delicioso* version that combines the best of both. And since it's 'shortcake,' let's keep it short, *mis amigos*, we have more goodies to make today!"

I look over at Javier, who is doing his best to bury his face under his mop of curls, until Tristan bops him on the head with his hat.

Frankie and I get back to making our plans as we follow Chef's instructions and cut up cold butter and start pinching it into the extra-light cake flour until it looks like grains of rice for our shortbread.

"I'm glad you think my idea is genius," I say, "but it's totally useless unless we can figure out how to make it happen." We mix in the rest of our short-bread ingredients: flour, sugar, and buttermilk. "To throw a party Liza would like, we need food, music, a place . . .

We gather our dough into a ball, knead it a little with some more flour, and then form it into a rectangle so that we can cut out circles. Then I line my shortbreads up in tidy rows on the baking sheet.

"And we can't do anything that would hurt Nana Silver's feelings," Frankie adds as we carry the cookies over to the oven.

The pound cakes are out, and most of them look golden and gorgeous—except for Frankie's mom's, which is flat and a little singed. I don't think Theresa has noticed yet, though, which is good. She always seems so sad when her things don't turn out right, and then she makes a joke out of it. I personally think her jokes are pretty funny, but they usually get on Frankie's nerves.

We have one last batch of cakes to make before

we start to decorate everything, and Chef Antonio tells us they're called *petit fours*, which means "small oven" in French. It seems to me that anything with a French name must be hard to make, but Chef tells us to have confidence.

"*Mis amigos*, remember that the key to pastries is in the batter. We just rearrange some ingredients, change the order a bit, and *voilà*, as the French say, we have a different confection altogether!"

"That's it!" I shout, before I can stop myself from saying it out loud. Everyone turns and looks at me. "I mean, that's such a great idea, you know, that you can make different things just by changing the batter a little bit." I can tell that I'm blushing, but for once I'm too excited to care.

"*Exactamente*, Señorita Lillian," Chef says, clearly pleased with my outburst, weird as it was. He turns to my mother. "She takes after you, Mei Yin—it sounds like you're going to have two wonderful bakers in the family." I'm pretty sure no one has ever referred to anyone in our family—the Wong family—as *any* kind of baker before. I make a mental note to use this as an example of irony the next time our English teacher, Ms. Bissessar, brings it up.

While we're whipping egg whites for the petit fours, I whisper ferociously to Frankie. "I've got it! We just change the order and the ingredients, like Chef said."

Frankie looks at me—is that admiration? I hope so!—and nods.

"We can make this party happen, we just need to figure out the right recipe."

Without making a sound, Frankie mouths: "You. Me. My house. Later." I smile to myself and do an imaginary little fist pump. Yes! As Frankie and Liza say when they do their little secret handshake: *Holla!*

We bake the petit fours in rectangle pans so that when they come out, we can cut them into little cake fingers and ice them individually. Apparently, they are *very* big at weddings and high teas, so Margo is more than a little obsessed with them.

Now it's time to make glazes for the pound cake (I do orange to match my orange cake. Plus I really like zesting!) and frosting for our layer cakes. Chef crammed so much into this last class that we're all zipping around the room with no time to chat.

I catch Liza's eye as she and Margo use pastry bags full of fluffy colored icing to add piping around their giant thirteen cake. I am sorry she hates this, but I'm getting really pumped up about the possibilities for her true party.

Tristan and Javier's iPod looks more like a stone tablet from ancient times, but they seem okay with that. Frankie and I agree that they look even cuter than usual concentrating on guiding the icing onto the cake. Meanwhile Frankie's mom squeezes the wrong end of her pastry tube and winds up with green icing exploding all over her face and hair. Even Frankie laughs as she helps Theresa clean herself off as best she can. "I always wanted some cool streaks in my hair!" Theresa chuckles, smoothing the green icing into her dark hair.

In the middle of everything, Angelica dances in from the back room spinning Cole around. They swoop over to Liza's table and check out Margo's idea of a birthday cake.

"Ah, Liza, *mi chica,* I feel so excited for your big party. Oooh, I remember when I had my *quinceañera* . . . I was such a wild girl, I just wanted to dance all night and eat everything in sight and it was just *maravilloso.* But then"—she clucks her tongue, looking at Chef—"I never got to plan another one." Cole giggles and she gives him a squeeze. "But, *ay Dios mio,* it was a beautiful night. . . ."

Frankie and I look at each other, dusted with flour and sugar and sticky with batter. She grins her big Frankie grin. "We are so totally going to do this," she whispers. "And I know who's going to help us!"

CHAPTER 23
Liza

The doorbell rings just as I finish zipping up the frilly purple poof-fest Nana bought me for the party. Dad's plane landed over an hour ago, but it can take forever to get from the airport in Queens to our neighborhood in Brooklyn. He texted me as soon as he landed, and I've been going over my plans for Operation: Family Reunion ever since. There's no time to waste—Phase One kicks off tonight.

The dress is what Mr. Mac would call an "icebreaker."

As soon as my dad sees it, we'll all start talking about how my grandmother is in full-on party control-freak mode and remembering other famous Nana moments. Then any weirdness or tension (a.k.a. "ice") between him and Mom will melt away, and they'll be on their way to getting back together.

Running in this dress is impossible so I speed-walk to the door. Mom is already on her way to answer it with Cole, who's tugging her along by the hand, but she stops in her tracks when she sees what I'm wearing.

"What's all this about, Liza Louise?" she asks, drawing a circle around me in the air with her free hand.

I shrug, but don't actually answer. She's seen the dress, of course, but I didn't tell her I'd be giving my dad a sneak preview so soon. "Should we let Daddy in together, Coley?" I say, bending down as far as my fairy-princess gown will let me and hoisting my not-so-little brother into my arms.

Cole plays with the layer of fluffy fabric that

wraps around my shoulders—"tulle," Nicole called it—as I open the door. My dad has a big smile on his face when he sees us both. He leans in and gives me a kiss and then holds his arms out, and I pass him Cole. My brother releases his grip on the tulle and spreads his arms as wide as he can before practically jumping into my dad's arms.

"Hey, big man, what's happening?" Dad asks after he catches his breath.

Cole turns and points a chubby finger in my direction. "Liza gettin' married!"

My dad and I crack up. My mom has been standing back by the sofa giving the three of us a few minutes alone together, but even she can't help laughing. Who needs an icebreaker with a crazy toddler around? The four of us have been in the same room for less than five minutes, and my plan is already working!

Dad puts Cole down on the floor and does his best to stop giggling. "Really?" he says, pretending to take my brother seriously. "Well, then I'm glad I came!" He puts his hand on my shoulder. "Lovely dress, Lize. When's the wedding?"

I shrug his hand away and give him a sarcastic smile. "Ha-ha. This is Nana Silver's idea of what's 'appropriate' to wear to a thirteenth birthday party." I step back and twirl around to show off the utter ridiculousness of the dress.

"Ah, that explains it," Dad says, giving me my-little-girl-is-growing-up looks. "I realize it's not your style, Liza Lou, but you really do look beautiful."

"Dad!" I stomp, making it clear that I haven't grown up all that much. "You're not actually going to make me wear it, are you?"

My mom and dad exchange a look. I'm not sure what it means, but I decide to consider any kind of eye contact a good sign.

"I just got in, sweetheart. Your mom and I will discuss the dress later. Right now, I just want to spend some time with you and Cole and hopefully get some food." He puts his hand on his stomach. "The only thing I've eaten since I left the West Coast was a bag of pretzels, and I'm starving!"

Since my dad just gave me the perfect lead-in to Phase Two of my plan, I decide to drop the dress thing for now.

"You know me, Dad. I'm always up for food."

"That's my girl," he says. "Where should we eat? Sushi? Indian? Italian? I sure have missed our daddy-daughter pizza dinners at Nino's."

"Actually, I was thinking all four of us should go somewhere. I'm sure Cole wants to spend more time with you tonight, and Mom, too." I catch my mom's eye as I say that and see that she's giving Dad another one of those looks.

For a minute no one says anything, and I realize this is definitely an "awkward moment."

"It's so sweet of you to think of us, honey," my mom says at last, "but Cole's had a long day, and he barely napped."

"Ooh, yeah," Dad says a little too quickly. "A

sleepy Cole is a cranky Cole—not the ideal dinner companion."

"I no need naps no more, Mama," Cole says, stomping his foot just like I did a few minutes ago and tugging at my mom's skirt.

Mom tousles his hair and gives one of his curls a little tug the way she does with my braids. "Oh yes, you do, Mister," she says. "And I'm the one who has to deal with you when you don't get enough rest. Let's let Daddy and Liza have a nice dinner together and you can see him again first thing in the morning after you've had a good night's sleep."

"Oh, come on, guys," I say, not ready to let my plan completely self-destruct without a fight. "It's only six thirty, and we're talking about Nino's, not the Four Seasons. No one's going to mind if Cole's a little grumpy."

"I NOT GRUMPY!" Cole insists, stomping on the floor with both feet this time, and proving that exactly the opposite is true. Is he actually *trying* to mess up my plans to get our parents back together?

Dad puts his arm around my shoulder. "I was really hoping to spend some time just with you tonight, Lize. You're the one who called me and asked me to come out early, remember? I want to hear all about Nana's crazy ideas for the party and catch up on everything else that's been going on with you." He looks up at my mom and then back to me. "And there's something I've been wanting to talk to you about too."

Okay, I'm confused. Mom and Dad have been acting like they don't really want to see each other— at least tonight—but they keep giving each other these weird looks. And now Dad says he wants to talk to me about something—alone. That has to be another good sign, right? Maybe what my dad wants to talk about is that he and my mom actually *are* getting back together, and he wants me to be the first to know. That would explain the weird looks, and the father-daughter dinner. I mean, when you think about it, what other reason could there be?

"Okay," I say, "table for two it is."

Dad squeezes my shoulders. "Thank you, sweetheart. That's great news," he says. "Now, how about we go get ourselves some pizza?"

"Sounds great," I say. "But, um, I should probably change into something just a little bit less formal."

My dad smiles. "Good idea. Nana Silver definitely would not approve if we accessorized your new dress with marinara sauce."

CHAPTER 24
Liza

Nino's is always crowded, but tonight it's even more packed than usual. There's a giant TV on one wall where most of the time they play old Italian movies with the sound off. Before the Big D (a.k.a. my parents' divorce), we used to have dinner at Nino's every Sunday night. While we ate our pizza, we'd watch the movie and make up what the different characters were saying (my English teacher, Ms. Bissessar, would call it "dialogue"). It didn't matter if they were

cowboys, old ladies, or little school girls, the characters would always be saying things like, "I love you
more than mozzarella cheese," and "You're my spicy
pepperoni"—even though no one in the movies was
ever eating pizza. My dad and I thought our game was
hilarious, and our pizza dinners often ended with me
laughing so hard that I choked on my Coke (the one
can I was allowed all week).

The only time the big TV at Nino's isn't showing
old movies is when one of the Italian soccer teams is
playing in a big match. Tonight is one of those times,
which explains why the place is so crowded. Luckily,
Tony D., one of the waiters who's been working at
Nino's forever (there's also a Tony R.), spots my dad
and me in the crowd of people waiting to be seated.
When he catches Dad's eye, a big smile takes over
Tony D.'s usually all-business face, and he waves us
over. Everyone gives us looks as we squeeze through
the mob waiting for tables, and I can tell they're wondering what we did to get the celebrity treatment.

I guess being a loyal customer for a decade has its perks, even if you move away and only come back to visit a couple of times a year.

Tony D. shows us to a table that has a great view of the TV. Dad likes soccer okay, but I can tell he's as bummed as I am that there's a game on instead of an old movie. We order our pizza—half pepperoni mushroom for me, half sausage and black olive for my dad—and a big Caesar salad to share. It might sound weird to get excited over a condiment, but the Caesar dressing at Nino's is almost better than the pizza. They say the secret is in the anchovies—they use a special kind that they import from some tiny town in Italy where the owners grew up. When I was little, you couldn't have bribed me with an unlimited supply of Barbies to even look at an actual anchovy, let alone eat one, but I would still happily scarf down a Nino's Caesar salad.

"They treating you good out there in Hollywood?" Tony D. asks when he brings us our drinks.

"Going to the beach every day and all that?"

Dad laughs. "Not quite, but I'm doing okay." He looks at me. "I miss having pizza dates with my little girl, though."

I smile, but I can feel myself blushing. My dad has gotten really mushy since the divorce. "I think he just misses the pizza," I tell Tony D. "We had some when I was in LA, and it's nowhere near as good as yours."

"So true," Dad says. "They don't know how to make pizza on the West Coast. I like avocado as much as the next guy, but I don't want it on my pizza." He squeezes a slice of lemon into his iced tea and looks up at Tony D. "If you guys ever want to open a Nino's II in LA, you've got a built-in loyal customer."

Tony D. grins. "I'll mention it to the boss. And I'll go check on your order before you forget what it's like to eat a real New York slice." He scoops our straw wrappers off the table. "Avocados," he mutters, shaking his head as he turns toward the kitchen.

"So tell me," my dad half yells over the roar of the

soccer fans on TV and in the restaurant (the Italian team must have just scored a goal), "I want to hear all about your crazy Nana."

I roll my eyes. "She's completely lost it, Dad."

I tell him about how she hired a car to take us all over the city to check out "venues," how she bossed around the really nice personal shopper at Bloomingdale's, and how she rejected the only truly pretty dress I tried on.

"And she hired some old-school caterer even though Chef Antonio—he's our cooking teacher— recommended a friend of his who does really fun, tasty party food, which is what I told Nana I wanted." I'm the one yelling now, even though the soccer fans have settled down. I take a long sip of my Coke. "And you've seen the invitations and the dress."

My dad runs his hand through his hair like he always does when he's frustrated. He has really thick hair that's just starting to get a little gray. Every time I see him, there are a few more gray hairs. He says he finally feels like a grown-up, because he's always had a boyish face.

"I should have known better than to trust my mother to keep her bossy streak in check. It's like asking her to suppress her entire personality." He sighs. "But I'm here now and I'm going to try to fix things. I'll call Nana tonight and insist that she meet me first thing tomorrow to go over all of the details. Maybe we can even exchange that dress."

With Dad clearly feeling guilty, I decide this is an opportunity to put the next phase of my brilliant plan into action.

"Why don't you come over to the apartment tomorrow and tell Nana to meet you there?" I suggest, in what I hope is a casual way. "We can all have brunch together, like in the old days."

My dad scrunches up his eyebrows. "You mean with your mom there too? She's been pretty clear about staying out of the party planning—remember? I don't think she'll want to be involved."

"She's making the desserts," I remind him. "Really good stuff, the stuff I like. And I'm sure she'll want to spend some time catching up with you."

My dad is about to say something, when Tony D. comes to the table carrying our pizza and salad on a big tray. Like all the waiters at Nino's, he makes a big production of slicing our pizza, and serves us each a giant helping of salad. Dad immediately picks up a slice and takes a bite, his face lighting up like he's just tasted heaven. Tony D. nods his head and pats my dad on the shoulder, satisfied that the memory of Los Angeles pizza has successfully been erased from his taste buds, at least for the moment.

My dad wipes a blob of sauce off his chin and comes back to earth. "Sorry, Lize," he says, jabbing his fork into the salad, "what were you saying?"

"I said you should come over tomorrow because Mom wants to see you too."

He does the scrunched-up eyebrow thing again. "She told you that?"

I shrug. "Well, not exactly. But she doesn't have to. Why wouldn't she want to see you? You guys have been talking on the phone a lot, right?"

My dad takes a deep breath and puts down his fork. "I'm glad you asked me to come out here, Liza. Not just so I can help with Nana and the party, but because there's something else I've been wanting to talk to you about."

Something in my stomach drops, like it does when you're about to go over the hill on a roller coaster. Is my dad actually about to tell me that he and my mom are getting back together? I hope I remembered to bring my phone so I can text Frankie and Lillian under the table the minute it happens.

I try to sound natural, even though I'm so excited I almost feel sick. "Okay, Dad," I say, hoping I sound like it's no big deal, "what's up?"

"Well, I've gone out on a few dates since your mom and I got divorced, but I never met anyone I felt like I could be in a relationship with. You know what I mean?"

"Uh-huh." Oh man, here it comes—the part where he says he's realized that he's still in love with Mom!

"Only now . . ." my dad picks up his pizza and puts it down again without taking a bite. It's kind of cute that he's so nervous to tell me about him and Mom.

"Only now I have met someone. We've been dating for a few months and things are getting serious, so I thought it was time to tell you. And hopefully next time you come out to visit, you can actually meet her in person."

Um . . .

Now I really feel sick to my stomach. For a second I think I might actually throw up right here at the table, all over our pizza and Caesar salad, and, if I'm lucky, my dad. Instead, out of nowhere, I start to cry. I've never been a crier, but I'm really sobbing now—not just a few tears trickling down my cheeks, but big, loud, ugly sobs.

All of a sudden, something happens that happens all the time in movies, but never in real life. Just as I'm starting to cry, all around us everyone in the restaurant jumps out of their seats, screaming and cheering. The Italian team scored a goal. Luckily, everyone is so busy being excited that nobody notices the weird almost-teenage girl hunched over her barely eaten pizza, bawling like a baby.

My dad jumps up and comes over to my side of the table. He tries to slide in next to me in the booth, but I don't let him. He tries to hug me, but I push him away.

"Liza, I'm sorry. I didn't realize you'd be so upset. I should have known this wasn't a good time to tell you, with all the stress about Nana and the party."

I wipe my eyes on a napkin and try to pull myself together. "It's not that," I say, unwilling to look my dad in the eye. "I'm not crying about the party."

Dad tries again to squeeze in next to me. "Come on, Lize, let's talk about this." I scooch over the tiniest bit, giving him just enough room to get one thigh in the booth. He takes it.

"I'm really sorry, sweetie. I didn't know the idea of me seeing someone would be so difficult for you."

"But you're supposed to be seeing Mom," I croak into my napkin.

"What?" Dad tucks my braids and a few curls behind my ear so he can see my face. I bury it deeper in the napkin. "What do you mean, Lize?"

I take a deep breath, but I still don't look at him. "You and Mom have been talking on the phone so much lately—and she's laughing and smiling more than she has in ages. I thought you guys were falling back in love, and that if you came out early and we did things as a family like we used to, you'd get back together."

My dad takes my hand. I try to pull it away but he holds on. "I'm glad your mom is smiling and laughing more than she has in a while, Liza," he says. "She deserves to be happy—but I can't take credit for that."

I peek up from my napkin. He's not saying what I hoped he would, but I want to hear more.

Dad squeezes my hand. "I want you to know that I do still love your mom, and I imagine that I always will. But I'm not *in* love with her anymore. I think that part is over. And I'm pretty confident she feels the same way."

I try not to let the tears that leap into my eyes roll down my face anymore. It's easier if I cover them back up with the napkin. "Does Mom know? About your relationship, I mean?"

My dad nods. "She does, Lize. I told her about a month ago."

Somehow I still can't put the pieces together. If my mom knew he was seeing someone, why did she act all smiley and cheerful when they talked on the phone?

"Do you think there's even a tiny possibility that you'll ever fall back in love with each other?" I ask. For some reason, I just need to know.

My dad shrugs. "There's always a possibility, Liza

Lou. 'Ever' is a long time, and who knows what will happen? But I don't want you to think that if you just try hard enough, we'll magically be a perfect family again. For one thing, we were never a perfect family. We might have looked like one on the outside, and tried to act like one for a little while after Cole was born, but your mom and I knew things were far from perfect on the inside."

Neither of us says anything for a while after that.

Finally, I pull my hand away. "So are things *perfect* with this person you're talking about?" I ask. "Are you in love?" I'm already dreading his answer.

"Her name is Helen. And no, it's not perfect. I wouldn't say we're in love—not yet anyway. But I would like you to meet her." My dad smiles, looking hopeful. "What do you think?"

I close my eyes. "I don't know," I say. "I don't really want to think about it right now. Ten minutes ago I thought we were going to have a totally different conversation."

"That's fair," Dad says. "Ten minutes ago I thought you asked me to come out early because Nana's been driving you crazy and making a mess of the party. Not because you thought you could kick-start a romance between me and your mom."

Even though I still feel awful, for some reason I chuckle a little. "Well, Nana *is* driving me crazy."

"Well, then, as long as I'm here, why don't you let her drive me crazy instead?"

I smile, in spite of everything, and finally look my dad in the eye. He pulls my head into his shoulder for an awkward side-by-side hug. I move over a little more so he can put both of his legs on the seat.

Tony D. comes to the table, and without saying a word he boxes up our barely-eaten pizza and pours our salad into a take-out container. He leaves the check and gives my dad a quick nod, which is his way of saying good-bye without disturbing our father-daughter moment. Unlike Nana Silver, I'm sure my dad is going to leave him a big tip.

CHAPTER 25
Frankie

I had a bad feeling when I woke up this morning. Really bad. It didn't help that one Goon was bellowing at the other Goon about a missing sneaker, but that was just the beginning.

The track tryouts on Monday are a bit of a blur, but once the relief of finishing them evaporated, the worry settled in to stay. I wasn't the worst one out there, but I definitely wasn't the best, either. For some reason, I couldn't summon any energy, any "pep," as my mom would say. I tried really hard, pushed as much as I could, even though it felt like I was running through quicksand. It wasn't even remotely fun. I think I did my best, though, and maybe that will be enough. I mean, it *usually* is.

The results are being posted right now—so I'm on my way to check out the bulletin board outside the gym before meeting Liza and Lillian for lunch. Then I can let them know the good news (I hope) while we're eating. Maybe they'll stop giving those looks to each other when I mention track. They think I don't notice, but I do. Liza's just longing for the old days when I hung out with her every day and complained about homework and goofed around. To be honest, I kind of miss those days too, but if Katie can push herself, I can too.

The list is already up. I can't see it yet, but the crowd of other would-be track stars is a dead give-away. Positive thinking, right? Dream it, be it, and all that.

Monica Langley is pumping her fist in the air. "YES!"

Guess she made it. But so what? She was really impressive at the tryouts, but just because she breezed past me a few times doesn't mean I didn't make it too.

"Good luck, Frankie." Monica smiles (or is that a smirk?) as she turns around. Forget positive thinking. I've hated Monica Langley since she locked me in a bathroom stall in kindergarten, and there's no question that was a smirk.

Luckily, I just have to get to the top of the Cs for Caputo, so this shouldn't take long. Okay, so Bacon, Beunosante, Bosolet, Carter, Cassina . . . Wait. Must have missed it.

Or not.

My ears are ringing with all the noise from the crowded hallway. Maybe it's under *F* for Francesca? But no.

I feel sick, but I try to keep my head up while I

walk away. No crying in public. I am not that girl.

I need to find Liza and Lillian, but they're probably out in the quad for lunch already. I'm not sure I can make it there without breaking down, so I text them both instead.

Two words. *No track.*

My phone immediately starts chirping with their replies, but suddenly I don't even have the energy to read them. I'm just so tired.

I turn off my phone and head to the nurse's office. When I tell her I have a splitting headache, it's not even a lie—I have headaches all the time these days.

I curl up in a ball on the hard little bed with its paper sheets and try to sleep. All I want to do is escape into sleep. If only I were like my brothers. They can sleep anywhere, anytime. Sitting up—even standing—it doesn't matter. Last year on the plane to Florida to visit my grandparents, both Goons just pulled their hoodies over their heads and said, "See you in Miami"—and they slept the whole way there. I'd trade my entire pristine Harry Potter boxed set to be able to do that right now.

But there's no way around it—I failed. I just wasn't good enough, I didn't work hard enough. I completely and utterly failed.

As soon as the final bell rings I race out of school without even bothering to stop at my locker.

I keep moving as I text Liza and Lillian. *Going home, talk later.*

I keep my head down as I get closer to my block, hoping I don't run into anyone. Of course, that's impossible in my neighborhood. By the time I make it to our house, I've waved halfheartedly at my kindergarten teacher, some retired friends of my grandfather's, Nicky's drum teacher, and the delivery guy from the grocery store. Finally, I reach our stoop and race up the stairs. If only I'd run that fast in the tryouts!

The house is totally quiet and I suddenly realize two things: I am home, all alone, for the first time in forever (which is amazing); and I am starving—totally starving. I'm hungrier than I can ever remember being—maybe hungrier than I've ever actually been. When I open the fridge, I spy a large container of Dad's gnocchi—his famous gnocchi, swimming in spicy marinara sauce and floating clouds of ricotta cheese—and before I know it I'm grabbing it with one hand and reaching for a fork with the other. I skip the microwave and start eating the gnocchi right out of the container, even though my mom would kill me. It tastes ridiculously good.

After a few bites, I actually start to feel better. Just like that. And then it hits me: I didn't fail. Not really. I just wasn't at full Frankie strength! I thought that if I ate lighter I would fly faster, but clearly that was the absolute wrong conclusion. Perfect Katie may float on the wind, all delicate and fairylike, but that's not me. I need fuel—tasty, energy-filled fuel—so that I can blast down the track. Next time, I'll do it my way.

I'm pretty sure that's a line from a Frank Sinatra song my papa Caputo likes to sing. Alone in my house, I start to giggle to myself, savoring every bite of my dad's delicious pasta. If he were here now, he'd be cracking up too.

I'm still digging into the pasta when the front door slams open, crashing into the wall and abruptly ending my peaceful moment in the kitchen. The Goons storm in, shoving and yelling, along with some friend of theirs. Before they even have a chance to say something obnoxious, I get up to leave, but they push their friend right into me.

"Hey, watch it, you monsters," I say. (Not one of my best lines, I know, but hey, I've had a rough day.) Then I make eye contact with the monster-in-question. OMG. It's Tristan. *Tristan Holland.* Total Hotness. Here? In my kitchen? What a heck? as Nicky likes to say.

"Um, hi," I manage, trying to smooth down my hair, which is all bed-heady from the hard-as-a-rock cot in the nurse's office. "What's up?"

"Yo, Frankie!" Tristan says in this loud, annoying voice that sounds exactly like my brothers'. He's snorting and laughing—practically grunting—just like they are and isn't even remotely acting like the cool skater dude I've been staring at every Saturday.

All three of them are yelling over each other about whatever happened at baseball practice (The Goons play anything that involves a ball). Apparently, it was so hilarious that the fact that I am standing right in front of him barely registers with Tristan at all.

"Wait a second," I holler over them. "You guys know each other?"

Leo finishes imitating a "totally awesome pitch" and then a *whoosh* over some guy's head and looks at me like *I'm* the idiot in the room.

"Uh, yeah, obviously. Tris plays D on our team. What's it to you, Frankenstein?"

I turn to look at Tristan, shoveling goldfish into his mouth and spitting out the crumbs as he laughs at something utterly stupid that Joey just said, and I realize that I feel nothing. No butterflies, no sweaty palms, no skipped heartbeats. Nope, none of that. Not anymore.

Tristan Holland, Total Hotness, my cooking class crush, is officially a Goon. And the girl who cared about impressing him is the same one who forgot who she was for a minute. Okay, maybe two minutes. But not anymore. I am *so* over her—and Tristan, and Katie. And so back to me.

CHAPTER 26
Liza

WHERE ARE YOU?

Frankie has been texting me nonstop for the past ten minutes. I don't blame her—if this were Frankie's party and she disappeared without a word, I'd be looking for her too. I'm surprised she hasn't found me yet, actually. I've been hiding out in the bathroom, inside one of the stalls, with my poofy purple dress practically spilling out of the space between the door and the black-and-white tiled floor.

It's a really fancy bathroom—much nicer than ours at home. It's probably the nicest bathroom I've ever been in. For one thing, it smells incredibly good—which I know is sort of a weird thing to say about a place where people, well, you know. There are two huge bouquets of flowers in here, but they must also use some kind of room spray that's so fresh and pretty you could wear it as perfume.

As nice as the bathroom smells, it looks even better. The counters around the sinks and beneath the mirrors are shiny black-and-gray stone ("Italian marble," Nana made sure to tell me), and they're so clean that they literally sparkle. All of the faucets and knobs, the frames around the mirrors, and even the pipes coming out of the toilets, are gold. They're probably not *real* gold, like the fourteen-carat kind, but they look super fancy, and in a place—I mean a *venue*—like this, who knows.

The venue. Surprise, surprise, Nana went with Buckingham Palace, even though she assured me my objections were "duly noted." The party room is just like I remember it from our visit, only it looks even more like a royal ballroom now with all the silver and china and frilly tablecloths (lavender, natch, to match my dress). Behind the giant parquet dance floor there's an old-fogy band playing songs I've never heard, and against one wall there are rows of buffet tables spilling over with elegant-looking (but totally boring) food. The one and only thing in the room that I agreed to is the table full of desserts that my mom spent every spare moment of the last week making. With help from Chef Antonio, Dr. Wong, and Theresa (though probably mostly Chef and Dr. Wong), Mom made every recipe we learned in cooking class this session. Our whole apartment smelled amazing all week—even better than this bathroom— and our refrigerator and freezer were stuffed full of delicious sweets.

I promised my mom that I'd wait until tonight to taste the desserts, and I doubt I'll have to worry about them running out—even though she agreed to let Mom handle the desserts, Nana decided (without telling us) to order a giant birthday cake, too. The bakery that made the cake has one of those machines that scans a photograph and prints out an exact copy in edible ink on top of the icing. Nana chose a photo of me as a toddler standing next to a woman's legs and holding her hand. You can't see the rest of the woman in the picture, but, of course, it's Nana. Her skin had fewer wrinkles then, but there's no mistaking her perfect French manicure.

"Liza, we know you're in here."

Frankie and Lillian have finally found me, but I'm not ready to leave my stall just yet.

"It's really nice in here, don't you guys think?" I call out.

They follow my voice, and two pairs of shoes appear beneath the door. Frankie's wearing shiny black pumps that Theresa takes out of her closet exactly once a year for the fifth-grade graduation at the elementary school where she teaches. Frankie's been wearing the same size shoe as her mom for a few months, and she was really excited to finally have an occasion to borrow this pair. If only she'd known that training for the track team equals major foot blisters. I can tell by the way she keeps shifting her feet that as pretty as they are, those three-inch heels are causing her serious pain. (Of course, I thought she'd be in some serious emotional pain too when she didn't make the team, but after her weird disappearing act that day, she seems fine about it. Frankie has never failed before in her life, but if getting cut from the team made her act like herself again, it's not really a failure at all, right?)

"You can't stay locked up in the bathroom all night, Liza," Lillian says. "You'll miss your whole party."

"That's the idea," I mutter, blinking back tears, because I am actually wearing a little mascara for the first time. I know that tears and mascara are not a pretty picture.

"Come on, it's not that bad," Frankie insists. "Did you see the buffet tables? There's enough food for the entire seventh grade!" Now that she's given up on training and gotten over her crush on Tristan, Frankie is back to relishing food.

"But there's hardly anyone from seventh grade here," I say. "Practically everyone in that room is over sixty, and most of them knew my dad when *he* was thirteen."

"That's not true," Lillian says. "We're here."

"And Javier, and Tristan, and Chef, and everyone from cooking class," Frankie chimes in. "Your parents are here, and Cole . . . A whole bunch of people came here to see *you*, Liza, not Nana Silver."

I look down at the two pairs of feet beneath the stall door and realize how much worse this night would be without my best friends. Slowly, I open the door. Free at last from the tiny stall, my dress practically explodes like an air bag in a car commercial, almost suffocating Frankie and Lillian as it unfurls in front of me.

"But look at me," I say, spreading out the purple poof. "How can I go out there looking like this?"

Frankie crosses her arms with her usual scowl and looks the dress up and down. I can tell she's trying to think of something—anything—positive to say about it.

"I'm not going to lie to you, Lize, it's a hideous dress," she says. I guess nothing positive came to mind. "But the good news is that it's so awful, no one who knows you will think you picked it out yourself."

I find that weirdly comforting. "But what about the people I don't know?" I ask. "Which is, I repeat, practically everyone."

Frankie shrugs. "Most of them are Nana Silver's friends. They'll love the dress as much as she does— and they'll think you have great taste for wearing it."

She has a point. But still . . .

"Did you see the band? They're, like, a hundred years old. And I don't even know any of the songs they're playing."

"They're actually pretty good," Lillian says.

I raise my eyebrows—are we talking about the same retirement home quintet?

Lillian rolls her eyes—spending so much time with Frankie and me is definitely rubbing off on her. "It's jazz. My father loves it—it's one of his secret American passions."

Frankie nods. "They're really pretty decent, Liza. You should see Chef—he's totally into it."

Chef. I'd forgotten all about the other reason I headed for the bathroom almost as soon as we arrived.

"Is he . . ." I feel weird saying this, even to my best friends. "Is Chef Antonio dancing with my mom?"

Frankie and Lillian exchange a look. "He wasn't when we came in here," Frankie says. "But I did see them smile at each other a couple of times. I know you don't want to hear this, Lize, but they make a really cute couple."

"So cute," Lillian echoes, holding her hand over

her heart. Could she be more of a hopeless romantic?

"What about my dad?" I ask. "Has he seen them, you know, smiling at each other?"

Frankie laughs. "He's too busy chatting with all of your grandmother's friends. He's doing a great job talking to people."

She looks at her delicate silver watch, which, like her shoes, is technically Theresa's. "Nana's probably going to come looking for you soon, Lize. No way we're the only ones to notice you disappeared from your own party."

Lillian nods. Of course, they're right.

"Fine," I sigh, scooping up the skirt of my dress so it doesn't drag along the bathroom floor—even though it's one of the cleanest bathroom floors I've ever seen. "Let's get this over with."

Frankie hooks her arm into one of mine and Lillian hooks hers into the other, and the three of us (plus my dress) squeeze ourselves out of the bathroom and into the party together.

CHAPTER 27
Lillian

I know this party is the complete opposite of what Liza wanted, but I can't help how excited I feel. Does that make me a bad friend? It's just that Javier looks even cuter than usual in dress pants and a button-down shirt, and he's been talking to me and Frankie a lot, since he hardly knows anyone else at the party. Tristan was invited too, of course, but he's been hanging out with Frankie's brothers the whole time instead of with Javier. I owe Liza a huge thank-you for inviting the entire Caputo family to keep Tristan entertained, so I get to see Javier, even if Frankie thinks The Goons are totally embarrassing.

I'm not a serious jazz fan like my father, but the band really isn't as terrible as Liza thinks. Some of the songs would be really fun to dance to, if you knew how. Frankie, Javier, and I have been watching Liza's grandmother's friends on the dance floor, and some of them can really dance! Javier keeps pointing at people and saying, "He's got the moves," or "She's got the moves," which cracks me and Frankie up every time. Coming from someone else, it might get annoying to hear the same line over and over—but Javier makes it seem funny and sweet.

I feel a little guilty for having a good time when Liza is clearly miserable. She's doing a decent job of pretending to be happy as she gets air-kissed by guest after guest, but it's not hard to tell that she's faking her smile. Frankie and I keep whispering to each other that it's okay that Liza's having an awful time at her not-mitzvah, because she's going to love her *real* party all the more, the one we've been secretly planning for later tonight at the cooking studio. As soon as we finish singing Happy Birthday and Liza blows out the candles, we'll sneak out and head back to Brooklyn to put our plan into action. In the meantime, though, I'm not in a hurry for this party to be over. Who knows whether Javier will pay attention to me later, when we're surrounded by a smaller group of people that he actually knows?

The band starts playing a song that must have been really popular once, because everybody recognizes it, including me—though for a million dollars I couldn't tell you what it's called. The dance floor is filling up with Mrs. Silver's—I know I'm supposed to say "Adele's," but it seems so wrong!—friends, who all really seem to have "the moves." I'm watching them spin each other around like they're actually twenty-five, not sixty-five, when out of nowhere someone grabs my hand. I turn around, and suddenly I'm staring directly into Javier's huge brown eyes.

"Lillian," he says, waving his other hand in front of my face. "Snap out of it and c'mon—let's dance!"

Before I have a chance to a.) ask Frankie if this is actually happening or b.) explain that I have absolutely no idea how to dance, Javier is literally pulling me onto the dance floor. As soon as we reach the other dancers, he starts doing exactly what everyone else is doing. He actually knows the steps!

"Wow," I say, just standing there watching, "where did you learn to do that?"

"Ballroom dancing class in fifth grade—everyone had to do it," he says, moving closer to me. "I can't believe I remember what to do!" Javier takes my hand again and tries to pull me toward him. "C'mon, it's actually fun."

I hold my ground. "But I don't know how!"

I turn back to Frankie for help, but she just flashes me a huge smile and give me a thumbs-up.

Javier laughs and gives my arm a yank. "So what? It's easy!" I lurch forward and am suddenly so close to him that our bodies are almost touching. I'm sure I'm going to either pass out or throw up, but instead I feel my feet start to move to the rhythm of the song.

If this were a movie, I'd magically know all of the steps and Javier and I would become the stars of the dance floor. Everyone else would spread out into a giant circle and we'd be in the middle, showing off our amazing skills while they clapped and cheered. Unfortunately for me, there doesn't seem to be even a drop of Hollywood magic in the air. My feet are moving, but not with any kind of a plan. By concentrating really hard, I'm able to keep the beat, but beyond that it's hard to say what I am doing.

For some reason, Javier doesn't seem to care. He just smiles—not quite as big as Frankie, but big enough—and does his best to lead me forward and backward and spin me around when he's supposed to. No matter what Javier said, this dance is *not* easy, and at first I'm too nervous and lost in concentration to think about anything besides how not to completely humiliate myself. But after a while I can feel the muscles in my face begin to relax. It's not that I'm suddenly becoming a better dancer, I'm just finally starting to realize that I'm actually dancing with Javier—in real life!

I would be embarrassed to be dancing with a boy in front of my parents, but, luckily, my mother is on the opposite side of the room. Believe it or not, Mrs. Silver has friends who are from the same part of Beijing where my parents grew up, and they've been parked at a table by the buffet all night figuring out how many people they know in common. Thanks to another major stroke of luck—my mother would say it's because today is the eighth, and eight is the ultimate Chinese lucky number—Katie isn't here to act all poised and perfect and make snobby comments, either. My father took her as his "date" to a boring faculty event at the university so she could have some practice talking to people who are even brainier than she is.

Javier is still smiling, and at last I've got the hang of this enough to smile back. I can tell the band is leading up to a big finish, but I don't have time to worry about what I'm supposed to do—Javier just grabs my hand and spins me around in a huge circle. I still have no idea what I'm doing, but when it's over, we're both still on our feet and no one seems to be staring at us, so I guess I didn't look like a total spaz.

Laughing and trying to catch your breath at the same time is hopeless, but that's what Javier and I are doing as we make our way off the dance floor. I can see Frankie watching us and snapping pictures with her phone. We stop at the table where we left our drinks, and Javier leans in close. Is he actually going to kiss me? Is Frankie going to capture the moment?

Javier reaches his arm toward my face and I start to close my eyes—only instead of my first real kiss, I feel a casual slap on the shoulder.

"I'm so glad we're good friends," Javier says. "I am always too nervous to dance like that at my school, but I don't have to worry about messing up and looking stupid with you."

My eyes are fully open now and staring hard at the floor. I can feel myself getting red all over, not just my cheeks but my whole face and probably my entire body. How could I be so stupid?

"Lillian? You okay?"

I can't speak. I'm sure even my tongue is blushing.

"I didn't mean that I don't have to worry about looking stupid because you look stupid," Javier rushes to say. He thinks I've turned into a human tomato because he insulted me. "I just meant I don't care about looking stupid in front of a friend. I do it all the time at the cooking studio, right?"

If there is anything lucky about this night, it's that before this moment turns even more awkward and humiliating, Frankie comes running over and starts frantically pointing to the birthday cake table being rolled onto the dance floor by two waiters.

"They're about to start Happy Birthday!" Frankie says in a whisper so loud she might as well be yelling. "It's Go Time!"

We all have our assignments: Javier, Chef Antonio, and Tristan leave first so they can open up the studio and move the big tables out of the middle of the room. Frankie and I stay until Liza blows out the candles. When the guests swarm around her with their happy-birthday wishes, we sneak out with our mothers to get started on setting up the decorations we spent the week making. Or at least, I did, because that's my thing. The Newlyweds, Henry, and Errol are in charge of kidnapping the desserts Liza's mom made and taking them to *our* party.

"Yes!" Javier yell-whispers back. "Let's do this!" He gives Frankie a fake-macho fist bump and tries to give me one too, but I pretend I need to retie the bow on my ballet flats.

I stay crouched down near the floor until Javier

leaves. If Frankie didn't yank me back up, I could probably have stayed like that all night—or at least until my lobster-red skin went back to its normal color. "I have no idea what just happened with you and Javier," Frankie says, smiling like there's actually something juicy to tell. "But I'm expecting details."

Explaining to Frankie that exactly nothing happened between me and Javier will have to wait until later. Mrs. Silver is calling us over to the cake table to pose for pictures with Liza while a waiter lights the candles. I hope I can rearrange my face into a fake smile.

CHAPTER 28
Liza

"Wishing you a wonderful year, Liza darling, and many, many more," Nana's friend Mrs. Markoff says as she plants a red lipstick-kiss on my cheek. I must look diseased by now with all the pucker marks on my face. "It was a lovely party."

Ha. I'm glad someone thought so. Or maybe I'm just the only one who didn't. Frankie and Lillian looked pretty happy the few times I actually saw them tonight. Now that everyone is leaving, I thought we'd finally have a chance to hang out—just the three of us, like the party I really wanted—but I can't find them anywhere. Would they really go home without telling me?

Nana Silver has been stuck to me like glue for the past half hour as I've been saying good night to her friends. After we kiss and hug and they tell me how beautiful my dress is (not!), nearly everyone hands me an envelope. According to Nana, there are checks inside all of them. After I thank each person for the gift, I hand it to Nana, who puts it in a pretty little bag she bought specifically for this purpose. I would be excited to scheme with Frankie and Lillian about all of the things we could buy with my birthday money, if I hadn't been told "in no uncertain terms" that practically all of it is going straight into my college fund. I guess Nana and her little bag are there to make sure I don't stash a couple of envelopes in my lavender ruffles.

"You see, Liza dear, the party wasn't so bad after all, was it?" Nana gloats when there's a break between good-byes. "Everything went just as we hoped it would, didn't it?"

"Yeah," I lie, "it was great. Thanks, Nana."

"I'm glad you enjoyed yourself, darling. I knew you would."

Just in time to save me from telling another lie, my mom appears, looking kind of frazzled. "Oh, there you are, Liza!" she says, and then gives my dress a tug. "Come on, it's time to go home."

Nana looks surprised. "Already? But our guests are still leaving—they'll want to say good night to the birthday girl."

"Well, they're just going to have to settle for a wave good-bye and a thank-you note," Mom says. "Cole's had enough—Adam's putting him in the rental car now."

"Well, if that's the case, Jacqueline, then why don't you take Cole home now, and Adam can drop Liza off later in a taxi?"

My mom doesn't respond right away. I can tell she's giving herself a mental pep talk to remain calm.

After a few seconds, what she calls her "professional smile" spreads across her face.

"It was so generous of you to throw this party for Liza, Adele," she says in that sweet but firm voice she uses when she asks a cashier if she can speak to the manager. "But it's been a very long day and it's time for us to go home now."

Nana sighs loudly. "Well, if you say so," she says, giving my hand a squeeze. "I guess you'd better go, dear." She reaches into the bag of envelopes and pulls out a perfectly square one that's the exact same shade of lavender as my dress. "But not before I give you this."

"What's this, Nana?" I ask, not quite taking the envelope from her. "You threw me this huge party— you don't need to give me a present, too."

"Of course I don't, darling—no one *needs* to give or receive gifts." Nana Silver presses the envelope into my hand. "But I want to."

Suddenly I feel a little guilty for how I've been acting—or at least how I've been feeling. If my grandmother knew the kind of thoughts I've been having about her lately, I doubt she'd be inspired to give me a present.

"That's so generous of you," I say. My mom nods her approval—she's big on manners. "Thank you so much, Nana."

"Aren't you going to open it?" Nana Silver holds up the bag of checks. "These can wait until tomorrow, but you should open that one now."

I look at my mom, but she just shrugs, so I follow Nana's lead, as usual. Carefully, I open the purple envelope and pull out the card inside. It's not a birthday card, and it isn't a check. It's way better: a gift certificate to Bubble Kingdom!

"Oh, Nana," I say, hugging her more tightly than I have in a long time—maybe ever.

Nana hugs me back. "You let me throw you the party I wanted, which meant a lot to me," she says, smoothing my curls. "Now you deserve to have the party that you wanted."

When we stop hugging, I show my mom the certificate. She smiles and gives Nana a hug too. "You know, Adele, you're full of surprises."

"Lucky girl—it's enough for three," Mom says. "Hmm, let me guess . . . You're bringing Cole and me, aren't you?"

Uh-oh, that wasn't my plan.

My mom starts laughing. "I'm kidding, Lize! You can call Frankie and Lillian from the car and tell them they've got a spa day coming up."

Nana puts her arm around my shoulder. "You're a lovely young woman with lovely friends, Liza. I hope you enjoy being thirteen."

"Good night, Nana," I say, hugging her again. She may not totally get me, but she really does totally love me. "Thank you for the party."

Once we're in the car and heading toward the Brooklyn Bridge, I call Frankie and Lillian to tell them about Bubble Kingdom. I get voice mail for both, so I try texting. No reply. For the first time since we climbed in the backseat, I look over at my brother, who's smiling and happily singing to himself in his car seat. "Not that I'm complaining at all, but why were you in such a hurry to leave?" I ask my mom. "Cole's not even crying yet."

She glances at me in the rearview mirror and shrugs. "I figured that it had gone on long enough," she says. "It was time to go."

"What happened to Dad?" I ask. "He didn't even say good-bye to me before we left."

"He went back up to the party to say good night to Nana and gather up your presents. He'll bring them over later."

"Presents!" Cole yells, clapping his hands. "Presents for Cole!"

Mom and I laugh. "No Cole-man," I say. "Presents for Liza."

My brother looks at me like I've just crushed his little heart. I give him a tickle under the chin. "But don't worry—if there are any cars, trucks, trains, or planes, they're all yours."

Cole starts clapping again, and I turn and look out my window. We're in Brooklyn now, but we're not taking our usual route home.

"Why are we going this way, Mom?" I ask. "Are we stopping to do an errand at ten thirty at night?"

"You could say that," my mom says, winking at me in the mirror.

Suddenly, I know exactly where we're going—the cooking studio. But why? Something strange is going on. Are my mom and Chef Antonio going to sit me down to tell me they've started dating—tonight? I take out my phone and text Frankie and Lillian again.

"What's going on?" I ask my mom as we slide into a parking space right across the street from Chef's studio (like that ever happens—a perfect parking space in Brooklyn!). When Cole sees where we are, he starts singing his favorite song—the one he and Angelica dance to every week. I check my phone while Mom unbuckles him from his car seat. Where are my friends? Why is no one texting me back?

When we reach the door of the cooking studio, my mom stops and looks me in the eye. "Liza," she says, gently smoothing a few of my fly-away curls, "happy birthday."

CHAPTER 29
Liza

You know that expression "I couldn't believe my eyes"? Well, when the studio door opens, that's exactly how I feel. There is no way to comprehend what I am seeing. Even though I come here every week, I hardly recognize the place. There are streamers and balloons everywhere. The tables are covered with beautiful, intricate tissue-paper flowers, and bright fluffy pom-poms—that I can instantly tell Lillian made—are hanging from the ceiling. A huge paper garland in her pretty script spells out *FELIZ CUMPLEAÑOS, HAPPY BIRTHDAY, MAZEL TOV* and is also hanging from the ceiling. And Angelica's Cuban playlist—the one we always listen to during class—is playing on the stereo. All of my favorite foods are piled up on the tables—Dr. Wong's dumplings; my mom's fried chicken and a pot of collard and mustard greens cooked with a ham hock; Frankie's dad's pasta with fresh tomato sauce, mint, and capers; Chef's rice and beans—and right in the middle are all of the incredible desserts that Nana had pushed away into the corner all night.

The studio looks, sounds, and smells amazing. Everything is perfect. And the best part is, I actually know everyone in the room: The Newlyweds— Margo and Stephen. Henry and Errol and Tristan. Chef, Angelica, and Javier. All of the Caputos, Dr. Wong . . . even the other Dr. Wong and Katie have shown up. My dad, who really did bring over all of the presents, my mom, and Cole. And, of course, Frankie and Lillian, who have crazy big smiles on their faces and who I'd bet every check in my bag full of envelopes are responsible for putting this all together. Looking around, I realize that knowing everyone in the room means everyone in the room knows me— the real me—the Liza Louise Reynolds-Silver me.

I'm pretty sure I'm going to start crying for the second time tonight, when Frankie and Lillian grab a big box from the pile of presents and hold it out in front of me. I look at them like they're nuts.

"Guys," I say, waving my arms around the whole room. "I don't need a present, too."

Frankie shoves the box at me, forcing me to take it. "Trust me, Lize, you kind of do."

Confused, I turn to Lillian, who is still smiling.

"It's not just from us, it's from our families, too. Open it, open it!" she squeals with a bunch of excited little claps.

I look at my mom, who nods. "Go on, Lize."

"I guess I have no choice!" I shrug. I unwrap the

box and hand the lid to Cole, who earns a big laugh by immediately putting it on his head. Carefully, I fold back the tissue paper.

It's the dress.

The perfectly poof-less, elegant, shine-free, midnight-blue dress that I tried on at Bloomingdale's. I hold it up to a roomful of "Ahhs." Frankie and Lillian beam.

"But how . . . ?"

"After the disastrous dress outing with your grand-mother, we knew we had to do something drastic," Frankie explains. "We called up Nicole—remember Nana Silver's personal shopper?—and asked her if the dress was still available in your size. She said she had a feeling she might hear from us again."

"She had actually put the dress on hold, just in case," gushes Lillian. "Can you believe it?"

I shake my head. I can't.

"Angelica helped us pull this all together," Lillian continues, "and we knew it would be the perfect time for you to wear it, so . . ."

"I can't believe it . . . ," I finally manage to say.

From the back of the room where she's been standing with Chef Antonio, Angelica walks toward me. "Well, believe it, *mi amor*," she says, her bangles tinkling like bells as she puts her arm around my shoulder. "Go put on the dress you love in *el baño*—time to get this *fiesta* started."

Angelica gives me a squeeze and then pushes me gently toward the bathroom as Cole jumps up and down at her feet. Hugging my new dress to my chest, I turn around to see her swoop him up as she always does and spin him over to the "dance floor" between the tables. Someone turns up the volume on the stereo, and soon everyone is dancing. I'm not exactly known for my impressive moves, but suddenly I can't wait to join them. If there weren't so many boys here, I'd start tearing off the hideous purple poof-fest before I even reach *el baño*.

CHAPTER 30

Frankie

Somehow, we actually pulled this alterna-mitzvah off without any drama or major disasters—I guess we've all had enough of both the past few months. You'd think with Tristan *and* Katie in the room, I'd be all kinds of stressed out, but I'm so over worrying about either of them. Watching perfect Katie nibble at her fruit salad all by herself, it hits me that I've never actually seen her look happy.

Sure she's cool and athletic and super smart—but if none of those things makes her happy, then she's not really perfect, is she?

It's still a little weird seeing Tristan with my brothers. All that time I was into him I had no idea that underneath his total hotness he was really just another Goon. Actually, it's kind of a relief. When he's not with Leo and Joey, he's pretty decent to hang out with. In fact, in honor of my new "enlightened sensibility," as Mr. Mac would say, I think I might just ask Tristan to dance. Who cares if I'm not *Dancing with the Stars* material—that's his problem, right?

Lillian

Seeing Liza so happy is almost enough to make me forget about Javier. Almost, but not quite. My cheeks start burning again whenever I think about how stupid I was to believe he might actually *like* me like me. Frankie told me that he's a boy and boys don't even realize what they're saying or how they're acting or what it might mean most of the time. She's probably right, but I can't help wishing my first real dance with a boy hadn't been a total misunderstanding. At least for me.

Still, despite feeling my heart deflate like a cartoon balloon, there was something nice about the way Javier said we were good friends—good enough that he feels comfortable just being himself around me. I mean, I've just spent the past six months being the new kid in school. If anyone should understand how huge it is to get to be your real self with real friends, it's me!

So, yeah, maybe tonight didn't turn out exactly as I'd hoped it would with Javier—but I have to say, I am still glad I danced with him. It was actually kind of cool, and excruciating at the same time. And everybody keeps praising all the paper flowers and colorful pom-poms I made (with no lavender in sight!), which is a great feeling. So even though Javier doesn't *like* me back, that doesn't mean we can't have fun together, right? He's out on the dance floor now with Frankie and Tristan, and he looks like he could use a partner. Now that my first dance with a boy is officially over, I might just be ready for my second.

Liza

My mom hasn't said anything to me yet about whatever's going on with Chef Antonio, but she doesn't have to. They've been side by side since we got here, first serving people food, now on the dance floor, and I can't remember the last time I saw her look this happy. It's definitely strange to think about my mom being with someone besides my dad, and I'd be lying if I said part of me wasn't still rooting for them to get back together. But even Dad is smiling, watching Mom and Chef dance—everyone is, actually—and if he can be happy for her, I should be too, right?

My dad just left me to dance with Cole and Angelica. The three of them look pretty adorable together, and I hope Stephen—who's apparently the official party photographer—gets some good pictures. I can't wait to *see* the pictures, because I'm definitely still overwhelmed by the all kinds of awesome that it took to make this party.

It's been about three minutes since the last time I thanked my incredible friends, so I think it's time I jumped onto the dance floor for another group hug.

So far, nothing about turning thirteen has gone as I'd expected—but it's been way better than I could have ever imagined. Who knows what might happen next? All I can say is that right now, thirteen is feeling pretty lucky.

ACKNOWLEDGMENTS

We want to thank our agent, Peter Steinberg, for his staunch support, advocacy, and enjoyment of a well-made cookie! We also thank our editor, Fiona Simpson, for keeping everything simmering along at a steady boil, with a consistent hand.

Thank you to our eager readers for insights and suggestions, as well as recipe requests. And to our families, who may or may not see aspects of themselves in these characters or situations, we are very grateful for a lifetime of inspiration. So to Deb's Lili, Julian, and Ian, and to JillEllyn's Eóin, Cullen, and Alan—you all take the cake! —DAL & JER